The Thinnai

Born in Madagascar, Ari Gautier has spent many years living in both India and France. He now lives in Norway, where beside his writing he is actively involved in the artistic and cultural milieu of Oslo.

A historian who specializes in the cultural exchange between France and India, Blake Smith has translated works by Pondicherrian author K. Madavane and Réunion-born poet Evariste Parny. He teaches at the University of Chicago.

Praise for the book

'Ari Gautier is among the greatest storytellers of our era, and his book opens up a world in which the symphony of cultures we discover will remain engraved in our collective memories.' – **Alain Mabanckou,** author of *Broken Glass* and *Memoirs of a Porcupine*

'This tour-de-force vividly evokes a Pondicherry of memorable characters, extraordinary travels, and linguistic nimbleness. On Ari Gautier's thinnai we encounter people and stories connecting Pondicherry to places across the oceans as well as to intensely local politics of race, caste, identity and belonging. French, Tamil, MGR, De Gaulle, Vietnamese snacks, Creole cuisine, all come together in a mix headier than arrack, washed down with delicious nuggets of Pondicherry's complex history. Savour Ari Gautier's witty yet melancholic prose, adroitly translated by Blake Smith, that evokes loss and recovery in equal measure. It will transform the way you see postcolonial South Asia.' – **Ananya Jahanara Kabir**, Infosys Prize Laureate 2017 and professor of English literature, King's College London

'Since nobody lives in the world in general, its unfolding can be observed from anywhere. Rarely will this be more rewarding than during time spent in the imaginary shade of a Pondicherry thinnai, in the company of Ari Gautier's vibrant cast of scoundrels, dreamers, nobles and loafers in this sensually lush, moving and hilarious yarn from a place of many worlds.' – **Thorgeir Kolshus**, Head, Section for diversity studies, Oslo Metropolitan University

'Never has there been a novel that treats French India from the perspective of the people who live there, making this novel a much-needed anti-colonial salve on an open wound. Gautier masterfully interweaves the lives of his characters, ranging from Franco-Tamilian soldiers to downtrodden white French elders to displaced Creole domestic servants, in order to bring out the complexities of the experiences of people who have been flattened by the historical record. Smart, illuminating, and often very funny, this is a must-read novel!' – **Jessica Namakkal,** author of *Unsettling Utopia: The Making and Unmaking of French India*

The Thinnai

Ari Gautier

Translated from the French original by Blake Smith

PAP TAGORE

hachette INDIA

First published in French by Le Lys Bleu Éditions in 2017

This translation first published in 2021 by Hachette India
(Registered name: Hachette Book Publishing India Pvt. Ltd)
An Hachette UK company
www.hachetteindia.com

SRD

The Work is published with the support of the Publication Assistance Programmes of the Institut français.

ISBN 978-93-89253-47-4

Hachette Book Publishing India Pvt. Ltd
4th & 5th Floors, Corporate Centre,
Plot No. 94, Sector 44, Gurugram 122003, India

Typeset in Bembo 11.5/17
by R. Ajith Kumar, New Delhi

MIX
Paper from responsible sources
FSC™ C043100

Printed and bound in India by
Manipal Technologies Limited, Manipal

To my father, who revealed to me the secrets of words.
To my brother Madi, who nourished my childhood with his stories.

Ari Gautier

To Margarita, from my little boat.

Blake Smith

TRANSLATOR'S NOTE

BLAKE SMITH

My relationship with Ari Gautier and his *Thinnai* began with a complaint. It was the spring of 2018, and I had just published an essay for the *Wire*, titled 'Indian Literature Speaks French', about the relatively unknown history of Indian authors writing short stories, poems and novels in the French language. Since the late nineteenth century, multilingual writers like Toru Dutt and Manohar Rai Sardessai have used French to express themselves, contributing to a small but diverse body of francophone Indian literature. Some of this writing was collected several years ago by Professor Vijaya Rao in a French-language anthology, but much of Indian French literature is still unpublished and untranslated. Outside of specialists like Professor Rao and her colleagues, India's contributions to the French language is hardly known in India, France or anywhere else.

Of course, no one knows everything, and most of us make do with knowing very little indeed. Scholars like myself often get very animated by the fact that something happens to be unknown – and we buckle down and try to make sense of it with the low, self-serving intent of being the first to write a little article about whatever unknown thing we have discovered, rarely asking ourselves if all the rest of humanity before us, which had decided such a thing was not worth knowing, might not have been right.

So perhaps the fact that French literature from India is 'unknown' does not signify anything to its benefit, and risks inviting to its table the worst sort of bookworms – the ones who will eat anything as long as it is obscure. Let me insist, then, that besides being off the map, it is also well worth visiting and includes some of my favorite poems. As I write this note, for example, I cannot help but think of these lines of Sardessai's poem, *Farewell, Paris*: 'I've been searching for words/ to fill up pages/ to make a book/ for some others yet to come/ for some other imbeciles.'

I had hoped my essay would draw attention to Professor Rao's work and excite greater interest in this literary field. More specifically and more self-interestedly, I also hoped it would generate some free publicity for *To Die in Benares*, my translation of a collection of short stories by the francophone Indian writer K. Madavane.

My previous efforts in this direction had been less than completely successful. An essay on Madavane that I had written for *Scroll* was given by the website's editors the title, 'This Indian author wrote his stories in French. Is that why we don't remember him?' This created the impression that Madavane, represented for the article in a rather funereal black-and-white portrait, was no longer among the living, and caused him to receive a number of anxious messages from friends and family. This time, I carefully ended the article with a mention of Madavane as a *living* author, and the hope for the survival of this minoritarian literary tradition.

But, in an effort to avoid making the same mistake twice, one can fall into a new form of error. An irate reader quickly noted in his comment beneath the article that I had failed to mention the new generation of francophone writers working today. The author of this comment – and, I soon learned, of two novels in French – was Ari Gautier.

As an academic and sometime journalist, I am used to making errors and having others point them out. Anyone who writes for a living is always getting things wrong! No great moral effort is required to be humble and magnanimous about my mistakes – they accumulate in such density around me that it would, in fact, be much more impressive if I were able, in a feat of willpower, to ignore their existence and maintain a superb self-image of my infallible intelligence. So I responded to Ari's comment, asking him to get in touch with me and to send me what he had written. I received his two novels (more are on the way!): *The Secret Diary of Lakshmi* and *The Thinnai*.

Both are 'Pondicherry novels', that is, if I can give a name to a genre of literature that, for the moment, does not exist beyond these two books. *The Secret Diary of Lakshmi*, which at the time I write this is being translated by a scholar in the United Kingdom, is the 'autobiography' of the resident elephant of Pondicherry's Arulmigu Manakula Vinayagar temple – and a critical fable about caste. Both charming and viciously satirical, the novel gives readers an elephant's-eye view of Indian society today. Being a historian by training, however, I could not help but be drawn to *The Thinnai*, which is, in a sense, the story of how a *thinnai* (a shaded verandah) can be a time machine.

The Thinnai begins with a meditation on memory. The narrator has returned to his childhood home in one of Pondicherry's northern suburbs, and notes with confusion and dismay everything that has changed (although some people have stayed irksomely the same) in his old neighbourhood. As he contemplates the thinnai of his childhood home, the novel takes us back in time to his youth, to a sleepy, village-like Pondicherry of ashramites, hippies and retired veterans of France's colonial wars. Readers meet the neighbours, and the tale moves back to their individual pasts and then forward into their present squabbles, couplings, rivalries and schemes. Then begins the story of Gilbert Thaata, the haggard old straggler who finds refuge in the narrator's thinnai and, night by night over many weeks, tells a family legend that is nothing less than the intertwined histories of the French empire and modern Pondicherry.

Everything is here: the rumors of rare gems that inspired peasant boys in Europe to take ship across the world to find their fortune, the difficulties and disasters of their journeys, the rise of colonial empires and the range of Indian responses, the families converting (with reservations) to Catholicism, the ones seeking a better life in other colonies as coolie laborers, the soldiers who fought for the empire, the Dravidian nationalists, the communists, the cynics. Four hundred years of history, crossed with journeys between continents, are held in a single picture by the frame of the thinnai.

In one of his verses, the poet Ghalib – whose philosophical depth is matched only by his passionate intensity – compares his gaze to the cord that binds the pages of a manuscript, and to a path unrolling toward the far horizon. He means by this that the separate sheets of our diverse impressions are held together in their proper sequence by the intentionality of a consciousness that projects itself forward in time and space. The poet's line of sight, transcribed in lines of verse, makes all things hang together in an intelligible world. In the sedentary universe of the thinnai, however, the wandering storyteller Gilbert Thaata only *seems* to play this part.

The thinnai is the real hero of the novel, Ari once told me. It is the part of the house that opens to the neighbourhood, the city, the world, the past, and is not just an empty space to be filled with whichever guests that may come along. The space is a plenitude, a living thing that draws history's infinite, indeterminate details into the order of a story. The thinnai is not only *where* the speaker speaks, but it is *what* he is speaking and *who* is speaking through him – it, and not Gilbert Thaata, is the vision and voice that puts things in their proper place. *The Thinnai* is the thinnai's story.

PROLOGUE

Once the house had appeared enormous. Now, beside the new grey buildings towering above it like unfriendly giants, it seemed a miserable shack. The old naga tree stretched its dry branches towards eternity, covering the roof with sickly yellow leaves. A funereal crow perched croaking on a wire. It flew away as I approached. Furtive shadows stared.

'Now play Sappani!' Emile Kozhukattai-Head's voice struck my ear like the crack of a whip. It was addressed to Three-Balls Six-Faces, who seemed relieved to see me. The latter stopped just as he was about to assume the role of Kamal Hassan, the crippled hero of *16 Vayadinilai*. He limped towards me. His smile flashed in and out of being as the broken lamp post flickered.

'These youths have no respect for anyone. Look what I'm reduced to: playing Sappani! To think I was once the great MGR; now I have to play Sappani the cripple.' Three-Balls Six-Faces began leaping joyously around me. He was grotesque. He hadn't changed. In spite of his age, he still wore the same torn shorts. His shirt squeezed against his body. Long, dirty hair fell down his broad shoulders. His face had the same old stupid smile. Melancholy seized me. I hardly had time to turn and look at the house before Three-Balls Six-Faces began his litany. 'Have you seen the house? Have you seen how things have changed in the neighbourhood? The ashramites are invading. It's sad, everyone's gone: Pascal Pig-Tail, Asamandi Baiyacaca Sonal's family, Joseph One-and-a-Half-Eyes, Pattakka, Selvanadin's family, Karika Bhai...everybody! I'm the only one who's left from the old bunch. Since your father left us, your old house has become a ruin.'

Like a lone warrior on the field of battle, Three-Balls Six-Faces regarded the devastation of the families who had left while he stood gloriously unconquered, proud of having survived. I hardly listened as I looked across at the neighbourhood where I had grown up. An austere pale-coloured house stood where Pattakka's hut had been, but the memory of her *kavapu*, *poritchundai* and bhaji drew me backward into the past. I closed my eyes and Pattakka's smile flashed like a mirage. To my left, Karika Bhai's shop had disappeared, along with the alleyway where the Killer Widow's house had been. Further off, a sign blazoned with great communist leaders hung in front of Manickam Annan's abandoned office. The playground near the coconut grove had been replaced by a hideous municipal garage.

'How you've changed! You're white as a *vellakaran*! You smell nice – like France! How long have you been gone? Two years, three years? How long will you stay?' Three-Balls Six-Faces loaded me with questions and paced around me, jealously patting my Ind-Suzuki. 'Can I take a spin?'

What a question!

'Do you know how to drive?' I asked harshly. After all these years, he still knew how to get on my nerves.

'No, but you'll teach me.'

Time should have forgotten him. I had grown up, matured, travelled over mountains and oceans. I had imagined that when I returned I'd find the same old huts, the same poor people stalking the neighbourhood with their memories etched in their faces.

'Who lives here?' I asked, looking at my old house, the *thinnai* looming in front of me. I wasn't interested, and I was afraid of a long, philosophical answer. Three-Balls Six-Faces pushed the motorcycle towards the house. He cast a disparaging look at the group around Emile Kozhukattai-Head.

Hanging from the dilapidated roof of the thinnai, by a strand of coconut fibre, an old petrol lamp swung from side to side, threatening to fall. It cast a wavering light over the jute sacks stacked against the wall, and on the books carefully lined up on a tiny shelf. Aluminium cups and plates were arranged by size; a plastic container nailed to the wall held silverware. Whoever was keeping up the thinnai must be someone tidy and well mannered. But who could be using spoons and forks in this part of town, and in our thinnai?

'Is Gilbert Thaata still...' My question hung in mid-air. I remembered that he had left the neighbourhood long before I did.

'You remember Gilbert Thaata?' Three-Balls Six-Faces asked with false admiration. I was familiar with the kind of flattery that praises the memory of someone returning from a long absence.

I took out my packet of cigarettes and sat in the thinnai. It seemed tiny. Even though it was dusk, I started looking over its corners and crevices, not bothering to respond to Three-Balls Six-Faces, who was now seated on the motorcycle and pretending to ride.

As if in contempt of the calendar, the thinnai had preserved its own mysterious temporality. From its nooks and crannies, dusty memories started to escape.

1

Gilbert Thaata came to our thinnai on King's Day, 14 July. No one could remember why the town celebrated the fall of the Bastille in this way, using the name of a long-forgotten festival. But, in spite of the anachronism, Pondicherry loved a holiday. It gave in to the joy of the crowd with a flag-waving earnestness. Everything that happened that day, each singular event, is carved into my memory as if with chisel and hammer.

Early that morning, Lourdes, our Creole servant, had lost her virginity under the ancient naga tree. Leaning against the tiny shrine at its foot, she had just given in to the persistence of Three-Balls Six-Faces, who had long been dreaming of this moment. My uncle caught him while he was still under Lourdes's upturned skirt. The guilty party scrambled up the tall branches. He leapt from one to another like a macaque, not knowing how he'd come down. My uncle tried to knock him off with a stick, insulting him with every epithet imaginable and inviting the members of his caste to go fornicate with primates.

In the house, my father had taken off his belt to punish Selvanadin's father, who cooked for us. He had just ruined my favourite dish, rabbit civet. Actually, he hadn't ruined it. He had simply taken the money that my father had given him to buy the meat and gone drinking; he had killed the neighbour's cat and passed it off as rabbit. After striking him, my father tied him to the foot of a coconut tree and let him roast in the sun.

Across the street, our neighbour Marie-Madeleine was giving birth to the child she had been carrying for thirteen months. Rumour was that it refused to leave her body. Some spoke of a curse; others blamed the solar eclipse. There was a local superstition that during a solar eclipse, pregnant women should avoid any sort of physical exertion. If by some misfortune a mother-to-be neglected to take these precautions, the child would be born with the tell-tale marks of whatever she had been doing.

The whole neighbourhood gathered in front of Marie-Madeleine's house to watch the miraculous birth. As a stained cloth was brought out into the street, the crowd screamed. The child had been born with a head as big as a watermelon. Not only was it abnormally sized, but there were fingermarks on its soft surface. After a second of stupefied horror, Marie-Madeleine's mother-in-law, bending over the filthy cloth, beat her chest and face as she shouted, '*Ayio, Tevudiya mundai!* I told you, I told you not to do anything during the eclipse of the sun! Did you listen when I told you not to touch the *kozhukattai*s?

No! You just had to make those goddamned kozhukattais for your grandmother – the toothless slut can't even eat them! Now look what's happened. Not only did you give birth three months late, but the child has a head shaped like a kozhukattai. How will I explain this to my son?' And so Emile Kozhukattai-Head was born.

While the young mother fainted at the sight of her child, a fight was breaking out at the end of the street. Bhuminadin's father, Pascal Pig-Tail, was chasing Edouard the Cripple with a bloody knife. Trying to escape his assailant, Edouard tripped over the inert body of Joseph One-and-a-Half-Eyes, who, drunk as usual, had collapsed in the middle of the street. Pascal Pig-Tail grabbed Edouard's withered leg, dragging it and its owner towards his hut. Edouard tried to cling to Joseph as Pascal brandished his knife and shouted, '*Tevudiya maganai*, give me the money for the *boudins*! If you didn't sell them, at least give me what's left; if not, I'll butcher you like a pig!' Bhuminadin came to his father's aid. Father and son began to drag the cripple and the drunk together towards their hut.

Besides his work as a road-mender, Pascal Pig-Tail made boudins and sold them on festival days. When he had a big order to fill, Edouard the Cripple would work for him. But the two men hated each other. Pascal accused his employee of stealing money; Edouard complained that his employer was dishonest. Welded together by a demon of fate, neither could do without the other. In spite of his wife's protests, Bhuminadin's father couldn't prevent himself from calling on Edouard the Cripple whenever he was overwhelmed with work. Things always came to the same end. Pascal would pursue Edouard through the streets of Kurusukuppam with his knife and a storm of curses; Edouard would try to escape, but after a few metres he'd be caught, betrayed by his feeble leg. It would conclude with a doubles match: the two fighters joined by their wives, who, after trying to tear apart their husbands, always began tearing out each other's hair. It was as if the two men had tacitly arranged the whole thing.

At first, neighbours had tried to intervene, separating them and trying to reason with them, but it was of no use. The two men would avoid each other like the plague, until their reconciliation at the next festival.

As soon as Edouard the Cripple smelled boudins, he shuffled like a zombie to Pascal Pig-Tail's house. He waited by the door, shuffling from side to side. Pascal sensed his presence, but kept haughtily silent. From time to time, he would sneak a glance at the door and order his wife, 'Tell that crippled bastard to screw off before I break his other leg. I don't work with thieves!' Edouard scratched his head; he wouldn't respond directly, but gave his answer to Bhuminadin's mother, '*Akka*, please! Tell him to give me one last chance. I swear on my son's head that this time I'll come back with the money. Every time I finish I go past that damn liquor shop, the devil tempts me and I drink up the money. I swear by Saint Francis of Assisi, it's the devil who makes me drink.' As he said it, he'd cross himself and turn a pitiful face to Pascal Pig-Tail. And so the routine began again. A few minutes later, Edouard would be heading off with a basket full of boudins; he would come back drunk, wobbling and ready for a beating.

Alerted by the shouts from the crowd gathered around Marie-Madeleine and by the moaning of Edouard the Cripple, my uncle dropped his stick to see what was going on. Three-Balls Six-Faces grabbed the chance to escape. Instead of climbing down the tree and running away, he had concocted a different strategy. The naga tree was enormous, with ancient branches stretching from the edge of our house and spreading over the neighbours' roofs. With his typical cleverness, Three-Balls Six-Faces imagined that he could make his way to the end of the branch on which he was perched, then slide onto the roof of his own house. Fate had other plans – the branch collapsed under his weight. Three-Balls Six-Faces dropped onto on our neighbour's palm-leaf roof, broke through it and flopped onto two naked, sweaty bodies.

'Ayio, ayio, *peyi, pisasu!*' As soon as she saw a dark mass falling from the sky, the woman began to scream. The man didn't bother trying to make sense of the situation; he took off running, naked as a worm. The terrified woman sheltered herself in a corner of the hut, pulling her sari from the floor to conceal her nakedness. As soon as Three-Balls Six-Faces was back on his feet, however unsteadily, he realized that he had landed in the house of the Killer Widow, whom he had been eyeing for some time. Taking advantage of her surprised and semi-clothed condition, he threw himself at her.

The Killer Widow realized that it was neither a ghost nor a devil who had come through her roof. She recovered her senses and readjusted her sari. Guessing what Three-Balls Six-Faces was thinking, she pushed him off; then taking a cauldron of boiling fish sauce, she poured it over his head and turned him out with a huge kick in the rear.

'Ayio, ayio, help! My head is burning!' Three-Balls Six-Faces shouted at the doorway of her hut. Then, picking himself up, he ran to the public fountain. His dirty, tousled head looked like that of Medusa, although instead of snakes there hung fish, cilantro and *karuvaipilai*.

Just at that moment, Velankanni, Three-Balls Six-Faces's mother, was squabbling with some women about whose turn it was to draw water from the fountain. The inhabitants of Kurusukuppam didn't have running water. Aside from Monsieur Michel and ourselves, no one even had toilets. The neighbourhood got water three times a day from the public fountain on the main road. The 'fountain', in fact, was just a metal tube sticking out of the ground with a faucet at the end. It looked like a submarine's periscope. Water came out of it early in the morning, between five and seven; then again in the middle of the day between noon and one; and finally, between four and six.

Women were used to lining up their jugs beside the faucet and patiently waiting for their turn. However, a day never passed without a new dispute; the women often came to blows. They walked home from the fountain gripping a clay jug in one hand and clasping their long hair in the other, firing the vilest insults with the fervour of a saint in prayer.

When Velankanni saw Three-Balls Six-Faces dragging himself to the fountain with a filthy face drenched in fish sauce, her jug fell from her hands and shattered. She grasped her son by the hand, shattering other jugs as she kicked them out of her way. She cleaned him and beat him in a single motion, not bothering to ask who had put him in this condition. All this multiplied the anger of the women with whom she had been arguing. Not only had she skipped to the front of the line, but she had also broken their jugs! What had been a mere argument was now a battle.

The women pulled Velankanni by the hair, dragging her away from the faucet, even as she kept trying to shove Three-Balls Six-Faces back under it. His screams of pain and the women's insults were eventually noticed by the neighbours who had assembled around Marie-Madeleine's house. They didn't know which way to turn their heads.

Selvanadin's father groaned beneath the blows of my father's belt, Edouard the Cripple took a thrashing, Marie-Madeleine screamed like a devil, Three-Balls Six-Faces cried in pain, the squabble around the fountain grew and grew, while Emile

Kozhukattai-Head started to cry, stifling his grandmother's curses. Crowded together like sardines, people moved from one attraction to another. In all the commotion, no one noticed a naked man running from the house of the Killer Widow.

The final bouquet was thrown from the house of Asamandi Baiyacaca Sonal. His real name was Jean-Noël, but the life of this ancient retiree, a relic from the Second World War, was a mystery. Jean-Noël had become Jonal and ended up as Sonal. Some said he was one hundred years old; others said that he was as old as our naga. Even my uncle, who knew everyone's stories, grew uncertain when he considered Asamandi Baiyacaca Sonal. The man's family simply retreated into an uncomfortable silence and lamented that he was still alive. Anyway, this is all pure foolishness, since in this neighbourhood time has never existed.

This old man's birth and early life, however, were a matter of consensus, having become one of Kurusukuppam's legends.

Contrary to what one might imagine, Jean-Noël had not been born on Christmas Day, nor in a stable. Rather, he had been born in a cowshed in front of his parents' hut. His pregnant mother had gone out to steal cow droppings so that she could make *erumuttai*s. The contractions had started suddenly and she gave birth in the excrement. Asamandi Baiyacaca Sonal's father, who had come running when he heard his wife's cries, realized what she had been doing in the cowshed. To avoid any suspicion of theft, he hurriedly washed her hands and ran through the neighbourhood announcing that his son had been born just like Jesus.

When the midwife arrived and picked up the child, she shouted with disgust, '*Asamandi Baiyacaca!*' What she meant was, 'My God, he smells like Baiya's shit' – Baiya being the name of the cow. Those who had gathered around the mother and child thought that this was the name the family had given him.

On the day of the child's baptism, the priest nearly lost his head as the father insisted the remarkable child be named Jesus Noël. The old curate refused, under any condition, to give the Saviour's name to this child born in cow dung. A few days later, he remorsefully baptised the child with the name Jean-Noël.

It didn't take long for the father – and everyone in the neighbourhood – to realize that the child had been born an idiot. Evidence of his unlimited brainlessness began accumulating even when he was still small. Not a day went by without Asamandi Baiyacaca Sonal's displays of imbecility earning him a beating from his outraged father. But this stupidity, everyone knew, could only be hereditary. From morning to night, Asamandi Baiyacaca Sonal, sore from his father's blows, would hide in the church, where his father never set foot. The old priest took pity on him, protected him and tried to give him something like an education. It was no use. Nothing stuck in the young man's head. He could spend whole days amidst books and resurface without having understood a word.

Physical proximity to holiness didn't stop the young man

from developing a taste for debauchery. It was hardly unusual to see him striding the streets of Kurusukuppam, drunkenly sweeping a lecherous glance over every woman he passed. The old priest didn't know anything about it. His father, relieved that his son was under ecclesiastical guidance, stopped beating him.

At least Asamandi Baiyacaca Sonal was a hard worker (unlike his father, who never did anything but steal from the neighbours). He wasn't afraid of using his hands. Built like a butcher, he could do the work of ten men, and in fact did everything that needed doing in the church. He was by turns mason, electrician, carpenter, cook, orphan-sitter and assistant sexton. The priest was satisfied, and even proud that he had managed to make something of this idiot. His joy was short-lived.

The blood nearly burst from the old priest's body the day the Mother Superior of the orphanage came to him in a panic. Several of her girls were sick, vomiting...pregnant! The old priest didn't know what to do. If he punished his ward, that idiot might set the whole neighbourhood talking. It would be a scandal; people would blame the priest. But if he kept Asamandi Baiyacaca Sonal on, that fool would turn his church into a maternity ward. That would be twice as scandalous! Cost what it might, he would have to rid himself of this libidinous cretin.

The old priest spent many sleepless nights not knowing which saint to pray to. In his nightmares, he could see himself thrown out of the diocese, forced to leave his beloved little church and, what was even more frightening, turned into the laughingstock of Kurusukuppam. Destiny came to his aid, in the form of a fellow named Charles André Joseph Marie de Gaulle.

On the night of 18 June 1940 in another part of the world, BBC Radio carried a message. Marshall Pétain of France had surrendered to the Germans. A week before, at the request of the French prime minister, Paul Reynaud, a young officer had been sent to London to seek help from Winston Churchill. It was Charles de Gaulle's first time in Great Britain, and he managed to get himself curtly sent back by the British prime minister. The future general returned to France empty-handed. Paul Reynaud resigned. Churchill, now realizing with a shock that nothing could prevent Marshall Pétain from forming a new government in Vichy and abandoning the war, helped prepare de Gaulle's escape from France.

On 23 June, seated by a window of his villa and gazing vaguely at its garden, Governor Bonvin was in the grip of a dilemma. His weary eyes could hardly make out the *aayi mandapam* that stood regally in the centre of the park, surrounded by the stately trees that he usually admired. He had lost his taste for contemplation ever since he had been wrested from his sleep by a messenger carrying a disastrous letter. It came from Colonel Schomberg, the British consul general, asking him to change his mind – earlier that day, Governor Bonvin had recognized the Vichy government. Although written by a friendly hand, the letter was a threat. Sunk in his distress, the governor didn't know what to do.

Three months later, on 7 September, Bonvin – having already notified Colonel Schomberg – announced that Pondicherry had joined the side of *la France libre*. To his boundless relief, the old priest learned a few days later that Asamandi Baiyacaca Sonal had joined the army and would soon be on his way to de Gaulle. He kneeled before the altar, spending hours in tearful, thankful prayer. God had spared him from shame.

While Governor Bonvin ardently read and reread the telegram that he had received from General de Gaulle, Asamandi Baiyacaca Sonal was leaving his neighbourhood, headed to the Rue de la Cantine. This street was filled with bars and restaurants popular with soldiers from the Compagnie des Cipayes. The young man often got himself food and drink there in exchange for various odd jobs. Sometimes he even managed to make a bit of money, which he spent on a prostitute to satisfy the demands of the flesh.

He was a kind of pastime for the soldiers. They generously got him drunk, then amused themselves by watching him fight other boys from the neighbourhood. He was not, after all, the only one that hung around the Rue de la Cantine looking for a few coins and free drinks.

The soldiers, who could sense their looming departure for the battlefield, were particularly open-handed that night. Asamandi Baiyacaca Sonal got drunker than usual, as he was solicited from every corner and ran in all directions to earn as much money as he could, stopping occasionally to swallow some whisky or other unfamiliar drink. Everything was going fine until a fight broke out.

Asamandi Baiyacaca Sonal had struck a soldier who had refused to pay him for some small service rendered. Several of the man's comrades unsuccessfully threw themselves at him. His strength multiplied by the quantities of alcohol he had imbibed, the young man was fighting like a devil. He not only freed himself from the soldiers' grip, but also snatched a bayonet that one of them had been holding, ready to attack anyone who dared approach.

Some soldiers ran; others stood immobile and stupefied by Asamandi Baiyacaca Sonal's menacing stare. He was making his way out of the bar, one backwards step at a time, when a bottle smashed against his right arm. He dropped the bayonet. A mob of soldiers fell on him. The last thing he could remember from that night was something hard striking his head, and a mixture of warm blood and whisky running down his neck.

When he awoke the next morning, he was bound hand and foot in a dark room in the barracks of the Compagnie des Cipahis. And so Asamandi Baiyacaca Sonal joined de Gaulle's nine hundred and fifty Pondicherrian soldiers.

From the day of his departure to the day of his demise, his military service remained a mystery. Nobody knew what Asamandi Baiyacaca Sonal really did during his years under the flag. The only thing certain was that he came back in a uniform covered with medals, and with a military pension. The rest were just wild stories. Some said he had been in the First Artillery Regiment of the Free French Forces. He had landed in Beirut, fighting in Egypt, Libya, Tunisia, Italy and in the liberation of Provence, after which he supposedly continued his service in a variety of colonial wars.

But he bragged to others that he had fought on other fronts, on every front. There were even rumours that he had been a spy entangled in all the intrigues of Levantine politics. These were mixed with sordid tales of theft, murder and fraud. Old Asamandi Baiyacaca Sonal never denied the rumours – which, it was suspected, he spread himself.

That 14 July – the King's Day and Bastille Day when Gilbert Thaata arrived on our thinnai – Asamandi Baiyacaca Sonal came home drunk, his ancient safari jacket missing one of its medals. When his first wife finally managed to pull a few words out of him, he mumbled something incomprehensible and fell asleep with his mouth agape.

Sonal had two wives, a number of children and innumerable grandchildren, all of whom lived in huts surrounding the main house. His first wife was a short-tempered woman. She seemed older than him and spent her days screaming at her husband and worthless sons. Sitting beneath the tamarind tree in their courtyard, her legs spread out in front of her, she pounded her pestle into the mortar, grinding areca nuts and glaring furiously at the men of the house. If she could, she would have ground them in her pestle too. Her betel-stained mouth was a well from which no one could draw anything but curses. She wore nothing under her sari. Her body, darkened by the sun, contrasted with her long cotton-white hair. Her earlobes dangled under the weight of the enormous gold pieces that Asamandi Baiyacaca Sonal had given her when they were wed. Her breasts hung like dried fruits on a dead branch.

Everyone could remember when, after several days' absence, Asamandi Baiyacaca Sonal had come home with another wife. The first wife had resisted, revolted and refused to let them into the house. Asamandi Baiyacaca Sonal and his second wife slept for a few weeks in the coconut grove behind the well. But he persevered; his back, swollen by his first wife's blows, did not bend. So the old woman adopted a different strategy. She acknowledged her rival and prepared a subtle vengeance.

Although Asamandi Baiyacaca Sonal was an old man, his second wife was young and lovely. The old woman, feigning kindness, encouraged her to eat plate after plate of succulent dishes. Suspecting nothing, the newcomer let herself be carried off by this wave of generosity. She was soon as fat as a stuffed goose. The beautiful girl, who had only shortly before been the collective object of desire for the neighbourhood's men, was now a motionless human mountain.

The old woman secretly rejoiced her plan's success. Asamandi Baiyacaca Sonal was miserable. He lost interest in his second wife and spent more and more time in the company of drink. People said he would have been happier if he put his muscles and brain to work, instead of the thing that dangled between his legs. But there was nothing that could be done. The old man spent his days running after *paavadai*s instead of working for his family. The old woman let him do what he wanted, as long as he didn't bring another woman home.

On that fourteenth of July, when he returned home with a missing medal, the old woman panicked. She was illiterate, but she knew each of her husband's insignia. He was missing his first decoration, his pride: the colonial medal from the Battle of Kufra. And while old Asamandi Baiyacaca Sonal fell in a heap beneath the tamarind, his open mouth a playground for flies, a young woman appeared at the entrance to the family's set of grass huts. When she noticed the stranger approaching with a bundle of clothes in hand, the old woman lost her senses.

No sooner had the fight at the well died down than the crowd was drawn by a new attraction: the screams of the harridan. The old woman shouted, waved her arms and called the newcomer every possible name. She beat her chest and threw handfuls of sand on the old man's body – which remained as placid as a corpse – as if she were trying to bury him. Her wrathful glare swept over the courtyard in search of something she could use to chase away the intruder.

She approached a pile of casuarina wood by the kitchen door, picked up a log and threw it at the young woman with a shout: 'See what my damned husband has brought me! See how the old pig rewards me for all our years together: a *koratti*! What kind of man from a good family could think of even touching such vermin; she sleeps with animals in the woods. Look how dirty she is! Lucky she didn't come with her box of *dalda* on her shoulders! And you, you bunch of useless idiots!' She turned now to her sons. 'Come here, come here. Throw this *tevudiya* and this old pervert out of here. I don't want her nasty feet dirtying up my house. If she steps inside, I swear I'll burn it down. I'll burn down all the huts, and you too. This koratti will never come in!'

The show's final act played to the amusement of the whole neighbourhood. People laughed and made indecent remarks about the newcomer. The body of Asamandi Baiyacaca Sonal – apparently lifeless – was covered in sand, but a few medals poked through and glistened in the sun. His grandchildren pushed each other at the doorway to get a look at the koratti while his sons pretended to move their father into the shade; in reality they were searching his pockets for money.

It was later discovered that Asamandi Baiyacaca Sonal – who was a familiar visitor to the *kallukadai*, the toddy shop, by the train station, inhabited by a community of Koravas – had traded his medal for the young koratti.

All the while, seated on our thinnai, I was calmly reading *Asterix*. Nothing could interrupt me. It had taken two weeks of bargaining and a thousand promises to borrow the comic book from Eric, the son of the director of the Alliance Française. Now I had to finish reading it before my brother borrowed it from me. But he was busy pacing around the roast chicken and worrying about whether he would get his potato purée – Selvanadin's father, after all, was still tied to the foot of the tree.

As I closed my book, with its final image of Cacofonix tied and gagged at the root of a mistletoe tree, I realized that Kurusukuppam was like the Gallic village in the comic.

2

Kurusukuppam, or Kurichikuppam. No one knew our neighbourhood's real name. It had started as a shelter for fishermen. Some said that the name Kurichikuppam came from *kurichi*, a flat, silvery fish about 20 centimetres long. There was an abundance of these fish in the *kuppam* – a village of fishermen or low-caste people. But others insist that Kurusukuppam owed its name to the cross, or *kurusu*, atop the church.

Kurusukuppam had only four main streets. The first, which passed from east to west, was an extension of Pondicherry's Cours Chabrol, but became a nameless road long before it got to us. Beyond it was the fishermen's shed, and the big house that had been built by Selvaraj Chettiar, the former head of the boatmen. Still further off was the village of Vaithikuppam. The second street was Rue Pappammal Covil, which started at Boulevard Nord and stopped in front of our church, Saint Francis of Assisi. The third was an extension of Gingee Salai that passed through Kurusukuppam and gave out by the cemetery. The final street, perpendicular to the other three, was Rue Avocat Chinnatamby. It ran from our house to Selvaraj Chettiar's. Insignificant little alleyways that the postmen were either ignoring or hadn't yet discovered made up the rest of this neighbourhood.

Like most of its other inhabitants, our family was not originally from Kurusukuppam. My great-grandfather had been the sexton of the church at Ariyankuppam. He had been transferred to the church of Saint Francis and given a little piece of land. My father told us about his ancestors, inhabitants of ancient Arikamedu who had traded with Greece, Rome, China, Thailand, Indonesia and Sri Lanka. On monsoon days, he would sit in the big thinnai and bring fabulous stories of Arikamedu to life as we watched the falling rain.

My father would begin by telling us about the coming of the Yavanas, the traders and navigators from the Mediterranean. I could stay awake for that. Once he began to penetrate the labyrinth of archaeological discoveries – those of Guillaume Le Gentil, Jouveau Dubreuil, Sir Mortimer Wheeler and Jean-Marie Casal – it was as if all the dust from these excavations got into our eyes and forced them shut.

When he saw that we were on the border of sleep's kingdom, he left the archaeological digs and set a course for the Egyptian ports of Myos Hormus and Berenice, where amphorae were filled with Mediterranean wine, olive oil and *garum* sauce. He put us on the backs of camels and took us across the desert; he embarked us in boats sailing south through the Red Sea. From the ports of southern Arabia, we'd sail to northwest India, or to the south, or even to the coast of Somalia.

Tired from all this travelling, I was always the first to begin another round of sleep. My brother would pinch and kick me, trying to keep me awake. He knew that the best part of the story was about to begin. He relished the moments when the brigands traversed the desert and the pirates crossed the seas. These were the moments of daring and danger for the Yavanas – what my brother had been longing for. While I put my head on my father's lap and stretched myself out, my brother could see the Yavanas, carrying armloads of gifts, coming through the curtains of rain.

Just as every other house in the neighbourhood, ours was built of clay and covered with a roof of coconut leaves. It was fairly big, with two thinnais by the door. They were the soul of the house. If there was anything our neighbours envied us, it was our thinnais, especially the bigger one. They were never empty. A neighbour or a stranger could often be seen sitting there, without our being bothered in the least. When she first began to work for us, Lourdes couldn't stand that such people, known and unknown, were occupying our thinnais. But she soon realized that they were a refuge for poor folks making their way down the hazy roads of life.

Once through the door, there was a sitting room with a table, four chairs and a magnificent bookshelf. The floor was uneven;

we put stones and flattened boxes under the table and chairs to keep them steady. On the right, a small shelf with an old crucifix, two candlesticks and an incense-burner hung from the wall, flanked by icons of the Holy Family and the Virgin Mary. On the left hung family photos and images of various saints. Three large and airy rooms stood at the end of a spacious courtyard, and on the left a little kitchen where a black sideboard was the only piece of furniture. A granite mortar and pestle leaned against the wall. The dishes were arranged in the sideboard, the shelves of which were covered with old newspaper that Lourdes made a point of changing as often as possible. The clay oven sat on the ground, amid piles of wood and dried cow dung. In the very back, on the left, were the toilets.

My father's cousin, a gardener for the Pondicherry city government, had planted sunflowers, bougainvillea and other flowering plants in the courtyard beside the palm trees that served as a wall. And off to the right there stood the majestic naga tree, a century old, with a tiny temple at its feet. In spite of his conversion to Catholicism, my grandfather had insisted on planting this tree as a tribute to his Naga ancestors. The sexton couldn't escape his old beliefs.

Kurusukuppam was one of the poor neighbourhoods beyond the city boulevards. A house made of stone would have seemed a palace among the hovels, some of which didn't even have doors. A piece of old jute cloth protected the privacy of the families who lived there. On rainy and windy days, it writhed back and forth pitiably, letting sodden, miserable sighs escape from within. The interiors of these houses were so small that their inhabitants spent most of their time in the narrow and winding dirt road rather than in their homes. Their houses were cramped, with no interior walls: there was a single room for the whole family. This room was often divided by a partition that didn't reach the ceiling, behind which the meals were prepared; it offered the illusion of having a kitchen. The bathroom behind the house was a shower tray, screened by coconut leaves. These cottages were so small that the men slept on the thinnais – or even in the street – to leave room for their wives and children.

To our right, in a house with a large courtyard, lived two brothers who spent most of their time arguing. The elder worked as a guard at the girls' boarding school, the younger was employed at JIPMER hospital. Everyone dreaded the end of the day, when the two men would return from work already half drunk. It took very little to set off their tempers and bring them to blows. Their mother was a mean-spirited old woman who could have been the sister of Asamandi Baiyacaca Sonal's first wife. She was constantly drunk herself. Seated beneath a neem tree, her days ticked by to the sound of mortar and pestle and to the scoldings and insults she offered her daughters-in-law.

In the house next door lived the family of Manickam Annan. Nobody knew quite what he did; not even his wife, who was too discreet to ask. He always wore a spotless white shirt, decorated with a pen that he carefully placed in his right-hand pocket; his *veshti*, white as his shirt, was never creased; it was skilfully ironed by the launderer, who feared Manickam Annan like the devil. People made fun of Manickam, and called him Mr Rin, like the brand of detergent. His hair was perfectly styled; he was close-shaven, and he took great care of his appearance. Manickam Annam was short, square-jawed, and muscled in spite of his age. He walked almost flirtatiously, lifting a bit of his veshti with his left hand to show off his firm calves, reminders of an athletic youth.

Manickam Annan had a madness for writing. All he needed was a passer-by to ask him for directions: he would grab whatever bit of paper was at hand and sketch a map. If his wife told him what was needed from the store, he would write it down on a bit of a Charminar packet. If someone asked him what date it was, he would scribble it in the palm of their hand so they wouldn't forget. One day, I asked my uncle why he had this writing mania; my uncle told me that he wanted to show people he was literate. He was obsessed with distinguishing himself from the ignorant people who filled the neighbourhood. But my uncle quickly added that Manickam Annan's pen was used more for cleaning its owner's ears than for writing.

'What's his job, Uncle?' I asked one day, curious about what he could be doing, since he never left the neighbourhood. We would see him seated in front of a tea shop reading the newspaper or wandering in Kurusukuppam's alleyways. He could spend hours sermonizing and advising anyone who happened to speak to him, passionately elaborating a better future for our unjust and painful world.

'Manickam? He's a communist!' responded my irritated uncle.

'And what's a communist, Uncle?' I asked, not noticing his annoyance. He looked embarrassed and didn't know what to say. He seemed to be searching for a suitable explanation. His forehead wrinkled up; his eyebrows rose and fell; his eyes watched the street in the hope of finding someone to free him from this uncomfortable situation.

'A communist?' my uncle replied. 'That's a rebel, running after a revolution that doesn't exist!' He abruptly left the thinnai, leaving me wonderstruck. Although I didn't actually understand my uncle's response, I felt boundless admiration for Manickam Annan. The words 'rebel' and 'revolution' were enough to make our neighbour seem like a character from a fascinating novel.

In order to lead his utopian revolution, Manickam Annan had fathered an army of Bolsheviks, to whom he gave Soviet names that nobody could pronounce. So the famous Martov became Mantope, Bulganin became Bolkani, Krushchev became Guchov, Kosygin became Kushni, and so on and so forth until the last, Molto the Zebra (Molotov), who was a cocktail of cretinism. Manickam Annan's perpetually pregnant wife always had another rebel in her womb, ready to join the Bolshevik battalion. She spent her days chasing her children and squabbling with the neighbours who complained about the savage characters of these future Russian leaders.

The street ended at the shack of Pascal Pig-Tail and his family, who were usually no trouble as long as Edouard the Cripple didn't start any. Our neighbour across the street was a sweet and gentle woman called Pattakka. With no husband, she struggled and worked hard to raise five children. She had four daughters and a son named Gandhi, whose birth had added another star to the illustrious firmament of Kurusukuppam. Besides the Bolsheviks and a half-naked fakir, there were also boys named Nehru, Mountbatten, Netaji, Benito and Adolf. Who ever saw such eminent men parading in such filth?

Pattakka's marital status was an enigma that everyone wanted to solve, but the truth of which they were afraid to learn. Whenever her husband came up in conversation, she responded that he had gone. With whom? Where? To heaven or elsewhere? The neighbours consoled themselves with this evasive answer and looked at her with a certain sadness. But everyone admired her courage. She worked hard and lived decently in a neighbourhood where it was easy to fall into bad living. She had a little stand in front of her grass hut where she sold idlis, dosas and appams in the morning, and made dishes for the evening as well.

Early in the morning, the street would awaken to the smell of the coconut chutney she served with her idlis. I especially loved the smell of the mustard seeds that crackled in curry leaves before she mixed them into the chutney. Seated on our thinnai, I would watch Pattakka's smiling face half hidden behind the column of smoke that rose before her. Pearls of sweat beaded on her face in the heat of the sun and the oven over which she was bent all day long. When evening came, the smell of kavapus, and bhajis of fish, shrimp and eggs, perfumed the neighbourhood. The locals and passers-by gathered around her modest stand and left with their hands full of food wrapped in newspaper.

The two houses next to hers were inhabited by two cooks. In one lived Britto, who worked for a teacher at the Collège Français, his wife, Marie-Madeleine, and his mother. In the other lived Selvanadin's father, who worked for the vice-consul, Selvanadin, his wife and three daughters: Amala, Kamala and Vimala. They were both excellent cooks as long as they weren't in the grip of drink.

Selvanadin's father had missed his true vocation as a magician: he could make anything disappear and reappear in a new form. His sleight of hand displayed itself whenever his steps stumbled towards the 'Ethylian' Fields, where cats become rabbits and parakeets became quail. When he was under the influence of drink, he would quarrel with his honourable employer and leave his place of work as the astonished guests stared on.

Britto, in contrast, was a sneak who hid his roguery with kindly smiles. He also had a knack for making the dishes he cooked disappear. But unlike Selvanadin's father, he didn't have a knack for making the dishes reappear in a new guise. His speciality was theft. In his wily hands, two kilos of pork vindaloo could be thinned down to one, with the rest evaporating into a tin he hid in the folds of his *kaili* to take back to his greedy mother. The art of theft was matched with the art of confabulation. A botched biryani would find a new identity, becoming a mysterious dish that only he knew how to prepare. All this enraged my uncle.

One day when Britto was just about to make off with a full tin of mutton korma, my uncle asked him to run a last-minute errand. Once he was out of the door, my uncle took his tin and seasoned the mutton with a generous dose of ricin oil. Britto returned and received his pay and thanks. Then, with a bottle of liquor and his korma, my uncle seated himself on our thinnai. He had hardly finished his first glass when the smell of the stolen food wafted from Britto's hut. A few minutes later, we saw Britto's mother, with her son and Marie-Madeleine behind her, running towards the coconut grove gripping her belly. A triumphant smile lit up my uncle's face. They slunk back a few minutes later; when they caught sight of us, they forced themselves to smile as if everything was fine. No sooner had they re-entered the house than they all hurried back to the coconut grove. The game played out all afternoon, as my uncle laughed and laughed.

The house at the end of the street belonged to Michel. Everyone called him Monsieur Michel. His house distinguished itself from all the others with a large thatched roof, more expensive than palm leaf. Cold and inaccessible, with its doors usually closed, it looked like a fortress. Monsieur Michel worked in construction; he called himself an engineer and real estate promoter, but he was only a *maistri*. The neighbours, however, were impressed by his self-importance and deferred to him.

Although they dressed exactly alike, Manickam Annan (who lived across the street) and Monsieur Michel hated each other. Both of them sported a veshti and impeccably white shirt. Both carried a pen in their pocket and coquettishly lifted their veshti as they walked. But Manickam hated Monsieur Michel's bourgeois manners while the latter hated the former's proletarian spirit.

After Monsieur Michel's house, the narrow street turned a bit to the right. There was the cluster of huts where Edouard the Cripple's family lived. Joseph One-and-a-Half-Eyes was his neighbour, as well as old Asamandi Baiyacaca Sonal with his two wives, many children and an innumerable swarm of grandchildren. Everyone remembered the day when an agent of the French consulate had come to update the voting registry. The poor bureaucrat spent most of the day with Asamandi Baiyacaca Sonal, who was drunk and in a mood for telling war stories. At the end of the day, the agent went home with a migraine and without a list of residents, swearing that he would never return to our neighbourhood.

My brother and I tried many times to count the members of that family. We always ended tangled up in names. On one particularly boring day, Manickam Annan noticed us as we were preparing once again to confront this Herculean task. He was delighted to have an opportunity to use his pen, and sat down beside us on our thinnai. He asked me to find a bit of paper; then he began to list their names.

After having tried a number of strategies, he soon realized that he had let himself step into a befuddling business. The pen stopped working, leaving colourless furrows on a paper already filled with scribbles. He furiously shook it, then held it up to his eyes, setting it horizontally against the sun to see if there was still any ink left. Finally, he gave us a wrathful glare, wadded the paper into a ball and threw it into the distance, ordering us to do our schoolwork and stop wasting time with such nonsense.

Life in Kurusukuppam condensed around our house. Pattakka had her idli stand across the way, the fountain was just a few metres away and the only shop in the neighbourhood was on the main street by the playground. Karika Bhai, who ran the shop, was the only foreigner in the neighbourhood. His real name was Amanullah, and he was a Malaysian-Indian. But he couldn't avoid getting a nickname any more than anyone else in the neighbourhood could.

Kurusukuppam's inhabitants had a mania for giving nicknames: Three-Balls Six-Faces, Edouard the Cripple,

Joseph One-and-a-Half-Eyes, Emile Kozhukattai-Head, Jean-Claude Cow Shit, Broken-Arm Perumal, Good Bald Jean. Usually these names marked some singular physical trait: Three-Balls had three testicles, Edouard limped and Joseph squinted; Emile had a head like a kozhukattai, while Jean-Claude's was big and flat like a piece of cow dung; Perumal's arm had been deformed by an accident and Jean was born bald... and so on and so forth. Poor Karika Bhai got his name because he was a Muslim with rotten teeth. The real names got lost in the maze of collective memory, leaving only nicknames that followed people to their graves.

The Killer Widow, for example, was said to have murdered her husband. She and her sister lived just behind Karika Bhai's shop. They each had their own hut, which gave them a bit of privacy. The Killer Widow's husband had supposedly tried to rape her sister; he was now thought to be buried behind her hut. But she insisted that her husband was a businessman who was very involved in his work and always on the road. No one believed her, but no one dared to challenge her story. The sisters' beauty and charm heated the imaginations of neighbourhood's men, who knew all their comings and goings. When night fell, cautious shadows crept along the little alleyway.

Unlike the Killer Widow, who didn't worry about her bad reputation, her younger sister, Suguna, was more discreet. Rarely appearing in public, she preferred the company of cinema magazines, which she savoured all day long. She sometimes went to talk with Karika Bhai and watch the young men playing football. Then she would make her way home, leaving a trail of sighs behind her. The two sisters filled the neighbourhood women – who never had the courage to confront them – with fear and disgust.

The men felt otherwise. They often crowded around Karika Bhai's shop, pretending to read the newspaper or smoke beedis. When Ramu opened a tea shop across the street, the men were euphoric. Now they didn't need an excuse to sit in front of the alleyway that they dreamed about so passionately. They kept their eyes fixed on the forbidden paradise, waiting for the objects of their fantasies.

Karika Bhai was at first annoyed to see Ramu setting up shop so close to him. He saw a rival who would steal his clients (even if he really didn't like having them crowd around his shop). But commercial solidarity won out. Pattakka, Karika Bhai and Ramu held a meeting. They decided that Pattakka would sell idlis and kavapus, Ramu would serve tea and drinks and Karika Bhai would sell everything else the neighbourhood needed. Karika Bhai was clever enough to give Ramu newspapers and magazines in a Machiavellian scheme to keep the tea shop's clients captive.

The real beneficiary, however, was Manickam Annan. He began waking earlier than usual, washing himself, putting on his spotless clothes and setting himself down on the tea shop bench before the other clients reached, when Pattakka and Karika Bhai were just opening their own shops. The smell of idlis mixed with the steam of hot tea. Stretching lazily, the usual customers made their way to the shop with sticks of neem between their teeth. While everyone waited for Karika Bhai's arrival, Manickam Annan readied himself.

Holding a newspaper in his hands, he asked Ramu for his tea (which, through a secret arrangement, he never paid for). As soon as those around him had fallen silent (he hated the sound of throat-clearing and people spitting; besides, it could get on his clothes!), he began to read. This reading session soon became a political rally, and Manickam Annan delighted in displaying his flair as an orator. Every article from the newspaper was followed by commentaries and observations such as he alone could make. Prompted by the desires of this old utopian desperately searching for a reason to live, the neighbours began to develop a social and political consciousness.

Until then, these poor people had been nothing more than a faceless bunch of ballots, ignored by the political establishment. Now they were becoming a voice. Overnight Manickam was transformed into the most respected person in the neighbourhood. Everyone rushed to seek his aid. Whether it was for writing letters to the government or correspondence to distant family, the inhabitants of Kurusukuppam sought him out. His pen had finally come alive.

Seated on the tea shop bench that had become his office, the man who had been so mocked and ignored was now enthusiastically writing pages and pages of letters, carried away by the lyricism of words. He could often be seen sitting on his bench with a steaming cup of tea, his pen tucked behind his right ear when he wasn't writing. Submerged in thought, he awaited the next poor victim who would receive a sermon on Bolshevism.

After a certain time, Ramu sensed a business opportunity and gathered his co-conspirators, Pattaka and Karika Bhai. They decided to give Manickam a little piece of land between the Killer Widow's alley and the house of Three-Balls Six-Faces. The three of them would arrange for a small public assistance office to be built, where Manickam could continue reading his newspaper and writing his letters. They went to see the neighbourhood *naattamai*, who lived near the bridge, and made their request to him. He didn't see any problem and gave them some land.

Once four stakes had been planted in the ground and four walls and a roof of palm leaves raised, Ramu placed a chair, a table and a bench inside. Manickam Annan had watched the construction distractedly, not suspecting that they were building his office. At the end of the day, while the workers sat on the tea shop bench drinking tea and waiting for their pay, the naattamai appeared. He sat down next to Manickam Annan, who was waiting for the evening newspaper and recounting for the thousandth time the history of communism to a passing drunk who was trying to buy some of Pattakka's bhajis.

When the drunk disappeared around the corner, mumbling of Lenin and Russia, the naattamai led Manickam Annan to the office. He said, 'Look, Manickam Annan, this will be your office. The neighbourhood is grateful for all your services. Since you started reading the newspaper and writing letters, people have realized that they're citizens too just like everyone else. So, thanks to my intervention and the contribution of these three benefactors, now you'll be able to right the wrongs for those poor people. But don't forget that I'm the one who had this idea, and that I'm still the boss of this neighbourhood.'

Manickam Annan had tears in his eyes. He ran back and forth from Karika Bhai to Ramu to Pattakka, shaking their hands and stuttering words of thanks before finally entering his office. He carefully placed his notepad on the left side of his desk, then on the right. Dissatisfied, he got up and looked at it from the perspective of a neighbour coming to see him; then he returned behind the desk and placed his notepad in the middle. He sat himself down solemnly as his three companions smiled. Three capitalists had just put a communist to work for them.

Ramu was right. In a few days, people flowed into Manickam Annan's office from morning to night. But whether it was crowded or not, Manickam Annan loved to make his clients wait on the tea shop bench. And so their torture began. They couldn't resist the smell of hot cardamom tea or the bhajis that Pattakka, with her eternal smile, was cooking. Then they heard the silent cry of the yellow Charminar packet and the beedis of Karika Bhai. No one could escape the hellish triangle.

One day, Manickam Annan pawned his wife's last jewel, and hired Siva – who worked as a graphic artist designing movie posters – to paint something for him. A few days later, the neighbourhood awoke to the sight of a joy-mad Manickam Annan ordering around some young men who were helping him put up a sign. The neighbours, who had been busy sipping tea and waiting for the day's news, were stunned to see the sign emblazoned with three heads.

No one dared speak during the installation, but when Manickam Annan had taken several steps back to contemplate his masterpiece, Ramu stepped up beside him and asked, 'Who are those three men? What does this all mean?'

The old communist turned proudly to the merchant. 'Ramu, thanks to you, no, thanks to all of you, dear friends, I have opened the neighbourhood's first solidarity centre. These three portraits you see are the greatest men the world has ever known: Marx, Lenin and Stalin! From now on, this place will be called the Communist Aid Bureau.'

Ramu had hardly counted on this. He didn't know what it meant. He stroked his beard and asked, 'Manickam Annan, I don't understand... Does this mean the office is only open to communists?'

'No, Ramu, of course not!'

Manickam Annan cut short the explanation he was about to give Ramu and addressed the small crowd that had started to form in the meantime. 'This centre is open to everyone. To all those who have been forgotten. From now on, I will be your spokesman; I will be the voice of the voiceless. I will fight for you! Your troubles are my own, comrades! You have nothing to fear. Together we can fight the oppressors and the government that ignores your problems. Together we will build a better future for our children.'

He waved his hands, raised his fist, put his hands on his hips and held out his arms as if to stroke the crowd. When he finished his speech, he sent the crowd off with a triumphant grin.

The regular clients didn't know what to make of such an event. Deprived of their usual reading, some stood with a dazed look and dangling arms, while others stared at the sign, trying to decipher who was who. Some doubters walked away murmuring that if Manickam Annan couldn't provide for his own children, how was he going to give a better future to theirs?

As he got ready to re-enter his office, Manickam Annan noticed that there was still one person watching him. She had stood there a long time, apart from the rest of the crowd. It was his wife. She stared at him, then turned her eyes to the sign. Here was the last necklace that she had managed to save, in spite of their miserable poverty. Her grandmother had given her this family jewel...which had transformed itself into a bushy head with a huge beard, a bald head with a goatee and a moustached head with a cap.

She turned her eyes away and took her youngest child by the hand. On the way back to her hut, she dried a tear with her sari.

3

By the time he got to Boulevard Nord, Gilbert Thaata was hardly able to stand. He was exhausted from the long march he'd started in Dupuypeth, where the lepers lived. Many times along the way, under the punishing July sun, he wished he hadn't started this journey. The pain in his foot started when he passed the church of Our Lady of the Immaculate Conception. He stopped for a few minutes at the corner of the Rue Saint-Ange to cross himself and to take a look ahead, feeling quite beleaguered. Pulling a dirty handkerchief out of his pocket, he wiped his neck and forehead. Then he asked directions from a passer-by, who answered with a gesture of refusal.

His left foot ached. Propping himself up on his cane, he continued on his way, careful only to put his weight on his right foot.

He stopped in front of Raghavan's shop, hoping to quench his thirst. There was a breeze wafting in from the direction of the monastery on the Rue Lally Tollendal, and Gilbert Thaata noticed that the Malayali shopkeeper was sound asleep, a worn-out fan slipping from his right hand. Annoyed, the old man looked around. A few hippies were sitting on the dais of the Modern Club, passing a chillum. They watched him mockingly through thick locks of hair that covered most of their faces. Unable to stand their glare, the old man turned his eyes back to the merchant. His dry throat bothered him, forcing him to cough. Awoken by the noise, the shopkeeper lazily opened one eye. With a drooping wave of the hand, he told Gilbert Thaata to look elsewhere. The old man continued his journey.

He passed the banquet hall on the corner of Gingee Salai and Rue Belcombe, where the smell of sambar and koutous floated by. 'It must be a Hindu marriage,' the old man thought. Men were standing around the door digesting their meal. Some were smoking, others spitting betel right and left beside garbage chutes overflowing with banana leaves to which bits of vegetables and rice still clung. Beggars fought over the leftovers while cows and crows perching on the backs of pigs watched enviously. Even here there was a hierarchy. First the beggars, then the cows and finally the pigs and crows.

Children in bright colours chased each other, shouting over the sounds of the *nagasvaram* and *tavil*. A few women in beautiful silk saris talked while leaning against the pillars. They were astonished at the sight of the old man covered in sweat. Gilbert Thaata didn't even look at them. He was ashamed of his appearance, which contrasted so starkly with the lovely, clean clothes those people wore. He looked like a forgotten scarecrow. To avoid the women's inquisitive stares, he hurried over the *pétanque* field that lay to the right. In spite of the heat, some boys were playing something like badminton with big wooden racquets and a rubber ball. Gilbert Thaata was relieved when he finally got to the clinic, the last building on Gingee Salai. His right arm was starting to hurt from leaning on the cane. He used his left to fan himself with his hat, which was as filthy as his clothes. His shoes had holes and hurt his feet. Sweat was pearling on long hair that looked like dirty snow. He leaned against the wall of the clinic. It smelled of urine and faeces.

'When will these people learn to use toilets?' he said, taking a disgusted look around him. 'And next to a clinic! If the sun ever does rise in India, the smell of shit will scare it away, that's for sure.' There was a poster on the wall for the family planning campaign *Naam Iruvar Namakku Iruvar* (We Two Our Two). The family of four on the poster hadn't escaped the pressing needs of passers-by. Streaks of urine ran from their eyes like tears.

Discouraged, Gilbert Thaata looked at the clinic's door. A huge lock hung on it. Propping himself on his cane, he stood on tiptoe and tried to see if there was anyone around. The clinic was deserted. It would have been so nice to sit under the mango tree and escape this infernal heat.

A few squirrels were running up and down the tree. They stopped briefly to stare at the old man, then resumed their play with sharp little cries. 'Kaa, kaa, kaa,' a middle-aged man called out to the crows, holding a dish of rice in his hands. They croaked happily and flew towards his voice. Gilbert Thaata watched the crows bitterly. The animals were happier than he was.

Putting his hat back on his head, the old man turned to search for Little Gilbert. The latter was a few steps behind him, towards the back of the building.

Little Gilbert had taken refuge in the shade of a bougainvillea that stretched past the clinic on the corner of Rue Perumal Covil. The sun was at its height. The boy was no less hungry and tired than the old man. He carried a bundle that was as big as he was. Exhausted, he set his burden down on the dusty ground and sat on it. He closed his eyes to savour, for an instant, the sweetness of the shade. He had hardly set himself down on the bundle when his back received a blow from the cane.

'Lazy, careless fool! Don't you see how dirty the ground is? Who knows what beggar or rickshawalla did his business here? You're tired already? After all you ate this morning? Go! Go ask the rickshawallas where to find the liquor shop by the tamarind,' the old man shouted, holding his cane in the air, poised to strike again.

Little Gilbert was caught off guard. He turned around and raised his right arm to ward off a second blow, then picked the bundle back up and moved towards the rickshaw stand. There were two rickshawallas sitting in a rickshaw with the hood raised to keep out the pitiless sun. A half-bottle of arrack stood on the little wooden bench behind the driver's seat. On the sidewalk, two women were preparing a meal. They had placed a battered aluminium container on a little clay oven. One was cutting vegetables while the other blew on the fire with the help of an *udankol*. The smell of meat and spices made Little Gilbert drool.

Another rickshawalla was learning drunk against the wall; his fingers still held a beedi. His head was bent to the side and his eyes were closed; he murmured something incomprehensible. He was shirtless. His body was painted blue, white and red: the colours of a country he had never known. A rivulet of drool flowed from the corner of his mouth onto his painted chest. Sweat and cheap paint left tricolour traces on the wall.

Little Gilbert readjusted his burden, then spoke to one of the rickshawallas. 'Hey, rickshawalla! Can you tell me how to get to the liquor shop by the tamarind? Is it far?'

The two men looked at the boy. One of them responded: 'Aren't you a little young for that kind of place?' Then he threw a suspicious glance at the bundle. 'And what've you got in there?'

Little Gilbert moved the bundle to the other shoulder. 'It's not for me. It's for my grandfather, over there.' He pointed with his chin to the old man.

The rickshawalla lowered his head. Looking through the bars that held up the rickshaw's screen, he saw the old man standing in the shade of the bougainvillea.

'Oh, the *sattaikara* Thaata? I know him. Anyway, I've seen him plenty of times! What's he doing here? And is he really your grandfather?'

'Listen, I don't have time to talk, and I don't have to explain anything to you. It's hot and the soles of my feet are burning. Just tell me in which direction to go, and how far. The rest isn't your business.' As he said this, Little Gilbert turned to face the old man, gesturing for him to be patient.

The rickshawalla didn't listen to the boy. He took his glass of arrack in one hand and sank the index finger of the other into a banyan leaf full of pickled citron. He swallowed his drink in a single gulp, twisted his face, put his finger in his mouth and smacked.

'Oh, calm down, little man! Aren't you smart for your age! The liquor shop is pretty far from here. At least half an hour's walk; with the old man, it'll take you an hour, maybe more. It's straight ahead – straiiiight ahead. You cross a little bridge, pass a little shop, you walk along the road of the Senganiammal temple past a rubbish heap, past a cemetery and it's just straight ahead. You'll see the tamarind, you can't miss it. It's enormous.' He pointed towards the road with a red finger, its dirty nail still streaked with pickled citron.

Little Gilbert looked in that direction. He sighed and turned back to the old man without bothering to thank the rickshawalla.

'Thaata, he says it's still far away! We still have another hour and a half of walking, maybe two,' he said, stamping his feet. Their soles were burning. His eyes were full of tears. He had lied to discourage the obstinate old man.

Gilbert Thaata let his arm slip from its place against the wall. His eyes scanned the nearby houses and the neighbourhood. Soldiers' homes flew French flags, which drooped wearily in the heat. It was so hot that even the asphalt was melting.

Some soldiers were coming back from the Bastille Day parade, proudly displaying their medals. Servants hurried to bring them fresh roti rolls and bottles of ice-cold beer. Bottles of Kalyani beer and Bagpiper whisky clanged together, teasing the old man. He could have strangled the sardarji who played the bagpipe on the whisky bottle's label.

A great sadness gripped him. He envied these men, these soldiers who had served France and returned to their country of origin young and rich. They were proud of having fought alongside the French, of having served the motherland. Happy to be back safe and sound, happy to have shared a destiny that united them. They no longer had to worry about tomorrow. Their pay was more than enough for them and their families. He could have been this one, or that one…he could have been anyone, anyone but this! At this old age, to wander without money, a home, a family, without anything!

His body sagged. His head was numb. He was about to fall asleep when a bicycle bell stirred him. He shifted more to the side as the bicycle whirled past. His dirty, sweat-stained safari jacket had left traces on the clinic's white wall. The sound of bottles clanging gave him a bit of courage and reminded him why he was travelling through this part of the city. He looked behind him, towards the road he had travelled. The Gingee Salai seemed as long as life.

He had to get out of Keerapalayam, a grim neighbourhood of quarrelsome fishermen and the weeping lepers. He had made his decision that very day, 14 July. He had to leave. He couldn't remember what had driven him to settle there. The old man had searched his memory and, finding nothing, had looked indecisively towards the road ahead of him.

He had stopped in front of the Nid Amical, not knowing where to go. He looked leftward; there was the brown-and-white Sacre Coeur church. There was a community of Christians living around it. With a little luck, he could find a charitable soul. But how would he find something to drink? There was always the liquor shop by the train station, but the sight of the Koravas who lived along the railroad didn't encourage him to take that path. On the right, there was only the fire brigade's headquarters, with some old colonial warehouses and a few scattered houses. Still further was the Park Guest House. But he didn't want to be with the Creoles. So he had walked down the Gingee Salai with no destination.

Halfway along the journey, he had decided to go to the liquor shop by the tamarind. He was thirsty. He needed alcohol.

His body and his head cried out for their daily doses of torpor.

He picked up the cane that was lying against the wall and said to Little Gilbert: 'It's just the same to me if the liquor shop's two hours away. We can't stay here in the middle of the street. We must go, even if it's at the other end of the world.'

'But Thaata, it's far, it's so far! And you're tired. You can't walk for two more hours. Why don't you sit there, and I'll go buy your liquor,' Little Gilbert said as he pointed out to the old man the area of the sidewalk where the rickshawallas' wives were cooking.

'Shut up, *chenapan*! You think I'm going to sit there on the sidewalk waiting for you? And with rickshawallas! Are you serious? Imbecile! Is this why I feed you, so you can leave me on the sidewalk with those rickshaw-driving dogs?' Gilbert Thaata lifted his cane to strike the boy again.

Little Gilbert stepped backward to dodge the blow. 'No, Thaata! I'm saying this for your own good! You can't even stand. Look, if you don't want to sit with the rickshawallas, at least you can sit in the shade of the temple over there,' insisted Little Gilbert. He pointed to the Kali temple a few metres away.

'You've lost your head, boy! Have you ever seen me step foot in such a place? A pagan temple! And to start with, nobody asked for your opinion...' Without finishing his sentence, he started across the boulevard. Little Gilbert could only follow. He readjusted the bundle on his sore shoulders and pursued the old man as the rickshawallas laughed. As they passed the temple, Little Gilbert cast an envious eye on the shadow of Kali's lion.

Following the directions that the rickshawalla had given, the old man and Little Gilbert came to the little bridge. The boy leaned his burden against the low wall of the bridge and relieved himself against a stationery shop. Without stopping, Gilbert Thaata continued on his way like a man possessed, driven by his desire for alcohol. His eyes were getting misty; his cane rattled against stones on the road. Nothing could stop him.

Little Gilbert retrieved his bundle and tried to catch up. The soles of his feet were burning; the load was getting heavier and heavier. He shifted it from one shoulder to the other every two metres. He didn't understand why he had to carry this enormous packet of dirty clothes and useless things that Gilbert Thaata refused to throw away. As he walked, he cursed fate for tying him to a mulish old man. Thinking about mules, the boy realized that he was the real beast of burden.

When he came to Karika Bhai's shop, Gilbert Thaata stopped in the middle of the street as if he had been paralysed. His head turned from left to right. By the time Little Gilbert caught up with him, the old man had taken off his hat and was sniffing the air. His halting breaths came faster and faster, like those of a drowning man struggling to breathe.

He gripped Little Gilbert's hand and said frantically, 'Smell, smell it, Gilbert! Tell me if I'm wrong! Isn't it French cooking? I'm sure, I can't be wrong. It's the smell of chicken – roast chicken, I say! Smell, damn it!'

The boy, who was happy just to stop for a moment, didn't listen to what the old man was saying. A moment later, he too was struck by the smell of cooking. The people buying groceries in Karika Bhai's shop were surprised and amused to see these two individuals behaving so strangely.

'Thaata, you're right! It smells like French food; I smell chicken and French fries!' Little Gilbert turned in the direction of the smell.

'You see! I was right. I'm not hallucinating. But who in this heap of huts could be making white men's food? I don't even see a French flag.'

The old man was growing more and more excited. 'Go! Go find out where the smell's coming from. It can't be far. I'll wait in the shade of the shop. But don't put the bundle on the ground, it's dirty here.'

Little Gilbert, who had been looking forward to unburdening himself, set off, disappointed.

He had scarcely taken a few steps before he saw a thinnai in the street on the right – a large, empty thinnai. His burning feet carried him there. 'I'll just set this damned bundle here, and then I'll go see where that smell is coming from,' he told himself.

Once the sack was on the ground, he grasped the soles of his feet and examined the thick, wrinkled skin that hurt so badly. Then he stretched his legs and made a few limbering motions. He leaned his back against the wall and cracked his fingers. He felt the fresh breeze that passed through the naga tree and closed his eyes, surrendering himself to the delicious shade of the thinnai. The idea of finding the source of that smell of good cooking had vanished from his mind. In an instant, this oasis had made him forget the old man, the liquor shop and the hunger that tugged at him.

It took a few minutes to remember his mission. As if awaking from a long dream, he got up and began searching the street. He turned in the direction of the sea, where the wind was carrying the smell of food. He stopped in front of Manickam Annan's house. But instead of chicken and French fries, he only smelled cod. Then he realized the smell was coming from our house.

Immersed in my book, I hardly noticed the boy standing at our doorway. I could make out his silhouette; but with all the commotion and everyone filing from one house to another, his presence didn't disturb me in the least.

Little Gilbert stood in front of our house for a few minutes. Then, when he was sure that the smell was coming from there, he went back to the old man.

'You took your time!' Gilbert Thaata scolded. He was standing in front of the shop with a worn-out expression and his hat in his hand. 'But where's the bundle?' Panic gripped him. Without waiting for an answer, the old man's cane struck the boy's back. Little Gilbert shouted in pain, which drew the attention of the shop's clients.

'But Thaata, I just found the house where the smell is coming from, and I put the sack on the thinnai,' the boy answered as he writhed. Tears of suffering and humiliation flowed down his dirty face, mingling with sweat.

'Oh? And how many times have I told you never to leave that bundle! It's all we have. What if someone steals it? Don't trust anyone, especially in this district of *mackoua*s and beggars!' People turned to look at the old man, intending to protest; but they took a look at his furious white face and decided against it.

Little Gilbert wiped his face with the back of his hand and led the old man to the thinnai. The old man looked around. His disappointment was obvious. When Little Gilbert said that he had found a thinnai, the old man had imagined a large stone house with a beautiful thinnai, like the ones that Chettiar houses have in Tamil neighbourhoods. His face fell as he looked at this clay house with its palm-leaf roof. He hesitated. But fatigue enveloped his body and pushed him to accept Little Gilbert's suggestion to sit down on the thinnai.

'Come on, Thaata, be reasonable. You'll be better off sitting here if you don't want to drop like a fly in this heat. Listen to what I'll do,' he pleaded. 'You sit down here and make yourself comfortable on the thinnai. I'll go buy your liquor. It won't take long; we're halfway there. And with a little luck, maybe we can eat some of this delicious French food. Look at that boy on the other thinnai – he's reading a French book,' he said, pointing at me.

Gilbert Thaata no longer reacted. His body sagged against the bundle, which was leaning against the wall. He closed his eyes to savour this moment of calm. His body relaxed, his muscles unwound and his head was suddenly empty. All the irritation, anxiety and obsessional desire for alcohol evaporated.

He fumbled in the pocket of his dirty safari jacket and drew out a few wrinkled rupees, which he handed to Little Gilbert. The boy took the money and asked the old man to step back a little; he dug his hand into the bundle to search for a quarter bottle. The old man looked at him.

'Take the half bottle, Gilbert. That way you won't have to go back there again tonight. You must be as tired as I am. Buy yourself something to eat. I'll take a potti curry and dosais, in case we can't get any food here.' The old man's voice had grown gentle, as if this thinnai had restored some of his humanity.

'Don't worry, Thaata, I'll come back as soon as I can. You want some water? Wait here, I'll go get some from the fountain.'

He took an old aluminium cup from the sack and headed to the fountain. He came back disappointed.

'Sorry, Thaata, there's no water. But I can ask that boy there, if you want.'

'No, no, I'll do it. You just need to go to the liquor shop. I'll talk to him and scout around.'

Little Gilbert ran in the direction of the liquor shop, leaving behind him an old man worn out by life. His sad blue eyes followed the boy's shadow until, at the corner of the Senganiammal temple, it disappeared.

4

Thambi! Thambi!

I thought I heard a far-off voice.

Thambi! Oh you, thambi!

The voice was becoming insistent, punctuated by the rattle of an aluminium cup dropped on the floor of the thinnai. I raised my head and noticed the old man. Absorbed in my reading, I had been unaware of his presence.

'Yes, what do you want?' I asked, quickly glancing at him.

'I'm thirsty, so thirsty. Could I have a drink of water?'

Without moving my head, I called our maid.

'Lourdes! Lourdes, come here!'

A voice came from inside the house. 'What is it now? I'm busy, you come here yourself.'

'No, you come here yourself. Someone wants water,' I shouted without budging.

'What a razor, this boy now!' Lourdes walked out from the house, drying her hands on her skirt. She looked displeased.

'Always talking me from outside. So now? I'm busy making clean!'

'Look, this man wants some water,' I told her, returning to my book.

She shot me an irritated glance and then turned to the thinnai. Catching sight of the old man, she stopped, mouth agape. Confronted with this unexpected silence, I shut my book. I was just as astonished as Lourdes to see a man dressed in a safari jacket, topped with a hat, clutching a cane.

He was no ordinary tramp. The colour of his hair and contours of his face made it obvious he wasn't Indian. But his skin resisted definition. The sun had browned and crumpled it, and a layer of dust and filth had dyed it an indeterminable hue. At some point, he must have been white. I suddenly realized the old man had been speaking to me in French.

We were used to beggars, the drunk and sickly passers-by who took refuge in our thinnai. But never a European. Amazed by this strange visitor, Lourdes stood with her arms dangling.

'Please, could you give me a glass of water. I'm really quite thirsty.' The old man doubled his politeness, sketching a smile and handing Lourdes his battered cup.

She took it, eyeing it suspiciously, and went back to the house. The old man, meanwhile, kept up his friendly smile and asked, 'What are you reading, young man?'

'*Asterix*,' I replied, showing him the cover.

'Do you like it?'

'Hmm, yes.' I hesitated. I was used to beggars and vagabonds who only spoke Tamil; I felt uncomfortable speaking French with this stranger. The only people in the neighbourhood who spoke French with me were my father, my brother, Father Trémond – the priest of the St Francis of Assisi Church – and, to a certain extent, Lourdes.

It was different with Lourdes. My father had forbidden her to speak to us in French, or rather, in Creole. That was her language. He would have preferred for her to speak in Tamil; he was afraid she would pervert our French.

Pondicherrian Creole is French compounded with Tamil and Portuguese words, spoken in a Tamil style. When she first started working for us, my brother and I had to make a desperate effort to understand her. We already juggled the French we spoke with our father and the Tamil we spoke with our uncle, aunt and neighbours. Now we had to add Lourdes's Creole. In a sense, it should have been an ideal language. This mix of French and Tamil could have been our family's lingua franca. But my father violently resisted the idea of Lourdes speaking to us in it.

As long as he was in sight, Lourdes would force herself to use Tamil. But as soon as his bicycle disappeared around the corner, she started up again with, 'What now... Razor now... Chatter this child now!' and a host of other expressions that only she fathomed. Lourdes didn't understand why my father forbade her from speaking this language; as far as she knew, it was French. She felt it unjust that he forced her to speak Tamil, a language she hadn't mastered.

Pondicherry has two distinct communities of Creoles: the High and the Low. Lourdes was one of the Low. Descendants of the French colonists – and speaking perfect French – the High Creoles disdained the Low for their Portuguese, English, Danish, Scottish or Dutch ancestry. The Low Creoles didn't live in the lovely colonial houses of the White Town. They were pushed aside – beyond the boulevards, into the fishing villages or the untouchables' slums: Dubrapayeth, Kurusukuppam, Uppalam. Pariahs among pariahs, they were ignored by Indians and despised by High Creoles.

This community confronted a racist society in an almost offhand way, strangely carefree and not without pride. They drowned their sufferings in the dance steps of a *chega*, singing Creole songs like '*Rousa Poudina*' or '*Marie le Pêcheur*'. Indians, for whom this nonchalance was inconceivable, accused them of being lazy good-for-nothings. They had a bad reputation: drinkers, dancers and revellers; they organized the town's masquerade.

Lourdes had inherited this freshness and lightness of being. Untroubled by the neighbours' mockeries and far from her community, she created a private world in our little kitchen surrounded by her recipes and photonovels.

We had known Lourdes for a long time. Her mother, Baby, had served us. No one knew Baby's real name. For obscure reasons, one of Lourdes's ancestors had been sent to India – one of a shipload of orphan girls intended for the Portuguese colonists. The dark fate that pursued her thrust her into the arms of a Portuguese officer. He took her to Madras and died. The widow, barely twenty, fled to Tranquebar, where she found a French adventurer in search of a European mistress.

After this, Lourdes's family history only re-emerges from the labyrinth of memory after the death of Baby's mother. At a very young age, she had left Tranquebar for Pondicherry, where she found work as a nanny for a rich High Creole family. Poverty and unhappiness hadn't weakened the girl's magnetizing beauty. She looked like a gypsy who hid in the folds of her skirt the secret of the *Thousand and One Nights*. The master of the house decided at length to uncover it. He abandoned his wife and children to set up the beautiful nanny in a big house on Rue Labourdonnais, where Baby was born. But the first wife's curse was soon knocking on their door.

Baby, the cherished daughter, married a scoundrel. Her parents died of shame. Her husband wasted their fortune in dubious affairs. He died in prison. The members of her father's first family took back the house and furniture. They left Baby and her three children in a hut in Uppalam. So she abandoned the children.

The two boys were admitted to the orphanage by the parish church; Lourdes was sent to St Joseph of Cluny School.

She didn't understand why she was being separated from her family. No one bothered to explain. She would spend whole days sitting on a bench under the plumeria, showing no interest in anyone. She spoke to no one, had no friends and didn't participate in anything happening around her. The nuns were at first concerned by the young girl's attitude, but they gradually forgot her. Lourdes was a shadow.

Each time she returned to the grey-and-white building after the Sunday walk, her heart shattered. It was the only walk in the whole week, and her only happy day. After the morning mass, she impatiently waited for the afternoon to end. She could hardly contain herself as the girls lined up and began to move towards the Cours Chabrol. She looked enviously at the Creole families chatting on the thresholds of their houses. From their rattan chairs, the Creoles savoured the evening's sweetness and gave the girls sad, knowing smiles. As she walked by, Lourdes heard French songs playing on old gramophones. They carried her back to her childhood. The familiar voices of Sylvie Vartan and Johnny Hallyday swayed her; she was once again in the strong arms of her father.

As long as she stayed inside the orphanage, such memories kept themselves hidden. But once she was in the street, her mind fired up, projecting images: a little girl ran alongside her father, off to buy chocolates in the Bazaar St Laurent. For her, the shops under the old arcades, where one could buy chocolate medallions wrapped in gold-coloured paper, were Ali Baba's cave. When she closed her eyes, she could still taste the chocolate. The taste was mixed with the smell of leather from the old workshop that had made her first pair of shoes. She could still feel the cobbler's heavy hands helping her close the buckle, and she could still see her father's radiant smile as she took her first steps.

All these images bustled in her brain down Rue Romain Rolland, down to the sea, moving to a cadence of the nuns' commands: 'Silence! Walk softly! Don't run! The sea isn't going anywhere!'

As she walked towards the beach, down the steps of the little square that surrounded the statue of Gandhi, her heart floated above the waves that leapt over the ancient pier. While the other girls played with the waves or gathered shells, one hand clutching their skirts blown upwards by the wind, she would sit down on a large rock. Over the crash of the waves, no one could hear her sigh.

When twilight fell, the moon came to whisper secrets in the ear of night and the waves quieted to a murmur. Then plodding steps brought her back to the grey-and-white prison.

That's how it was on Sundays.

Baby died during a cyclone. The funeral home's employees dragged the coffin towards the cemetery under a strong wind that bent the trees. After the funeral, Lourdes saw her brothers off as they returned to their orphanage. She dreaded going back to the nuns. A few hours before, she had asked my father if she could take her mother's place as our servant. She was anxiously awaiting his decision. The girl's persistence overcame my father's perplexity, and Lourdes, with great relief, left the orphanage.

Baby had hardly been able to cook an egg, but Lourdes knew the knack of Creole cuisine. Her spoon transformed the narrow kitchen into a culinary paradise, where one could taste the finest *baffade*: chicken marinated in a coconut milk sauce, expertly seasoned with cloves, cardamom, poppy seeds, cashew nuts, ghee and Kashmiri pepper. Her *fougade* – with sautéed vegetables, shrimp and grated coconut – could wake the dead. In Kurusukuppam it was said that the monsoon came just to taste her multani, which she started to prepare as soon as she saw dark clouds swell with rain. The fresh breeze that caressed the leaves of our naga tree carried the aroma through the neighbourhood. Seated in our thinnai, we savoured her soup as we watched the steam rising from our bowls and fading into the drizzle.

Before Lourdes came to our house, my father had always called on Khader Bhai, the town favourite, to make his famous Hyderabadi biryani. Khader Bhai belonged to a family of chefs that had once served the Nizam of Hyderabad. His imposing height, flowing beard and surly character were notorious in Pondicherry and all the surrounding areas. His prestige was such that he travelled exclusively in a private car.

A few months after Lourdes's arrival, my father called on Khader Bhai again. She was not at all impressed by the august master of biryani. His high-and-mighty airs irritated her so much that she challenged him to a contest. He was in an unusually good mood that day; amused by her insolence, he accepted. How could he have known that her old uncle had taught her the recipe for Bhatkali biryani, jealously guarded by the Muslims of Nawayath? The jury was unanimous. The little orphan had beaten the illustrious royal chef, who was never seen again.

The unhappy years in the orphanage were long behind her. She soon became part of our family. Besides the two brothers she visited every Sunday, she only had us. Once she left the convent, she became what she had been before: a joyful, generous girl overflowing with life. But she didn't let anyone step on her toes.

My father had imagined that he was only hiring her as a stopgap. But he soon realized that Lourdes had no intention of ever leaving. One day, after the subject had been broached to him by my aunt, he asked Lourdes about the prospect of her getting married. She turned scarlet and exploded: 'What? Monsieur, you want to marriage me? So why now? You know what tenderness I have for the children. I won't marriage myself to no *paya* from the street! Now, my cousin he called me from France. I'll go in the airplane and live with a white man, sir. What nerve now!'

My father never raised the topic again. There was, he knew, no cousin in France or anywhere else.

When Lourdes returned holding the cup filled with water, Gilbert Thaata was flipping the pages of *Asterix*. If he had been a normal passer-by, she would have set the cup down and returned to work. But given the singular strangeness of this visitor, she waited for him to raise his head. He thanked her with a friendly smile and drank the water. A few drops fell on his long beard. He dried them, stretched and handed me the book.

'Do you want more, Grandpa?' Lourdes asked.

'No, thank you, child,' he answered, putting his cup down. 'Tell me, are you Creole? What's your name?'

Lourdes's face lit up. It was rare that she could call her people by their name. The Tamils referred to them with epithets like *naatakavaii* (dirty skirts), *piitasattaykarichi* (fake whites) or *ding-dings*, a reference to the Anglo-Indian dish of dried meat.

'Yes, Grandpa, I'm Creole. My name is Lourdes, Lourdes de Mascarenhas,' she proudly replied.

She was on the verge of asking him something, but decided against it. The old man was pleased with her answer and continued, stroking his beard.

'And what's this? Is this a soldier's house?'

'Yes, Grandpa. Monsieur's a soldier, and he has two children. They go to the French school.'

'Are they nice?'

'Who, Grandpa?'

'The children, I mean.' The old man looked in my direction.

'Oh yes! They respect their father and they obey very good.'

Gilbert Thaata only half listened. Hunger tugged inside him and he wondered how he could turn the conversation to the subject of food. Lourdes was about to go back into the house, but afraid of seeming impolite, she hesitated, swaying by the door.

The old man let loose. 'And it's you who makes these tasty dishes? It smells so good!'

'Oh no, Grandpa. Today's special. It's the cook today. Anyway, sir just fought the cook, because he was making mischief. But me too I make good food. I make food in the evening,' she said, delighted to continue the conversation. She so wanted to ask the questions that were smouldering on her lips. Who was he? Where did he come from? What was he doing in this part of town? But she didn't dare.

'I have to go now, Grandpa. You need something else? I have to go start to make the table. Sir coming back now,' she said regretfully.

Disheartened, Gilbert Thaata watched her re-enter the house. He would have to wait to speak with her master. He pushed himself away from the bundle he had been leaning against. Picking himself up with both hands, he set himself on the edge of the thinnai and let his legs swing. His eyes turned to his shoes, full of holes. He stared at them with a pained smile and muttered to himself. The muttering became a monologue.

I left the old man with his invisible demons and went inside. Selvanadin's father had finished the roast chicken and was waiting on the rabbits, praying that they would be ready soon. He couldn't bear any more punishment from my father.

Before leaving, my father had sent Kaatannan to the Great Bazaar to buy rabbits. But Kaatannan still hadn't returned. His task must have been a difficult one, given how late in the day it now was. His long, lazy legs must be dragging themselves through the little passages of the butchers' corner of the market, which he knew like the inside of his pocket.

My father was in a bad mood.

It had started early. Lourdes had her daily dispute with the milkman. In spite of my father's warning, the girl couldn't keep from fighting with him. It was as if she had a physical need for a morning quarrel. The milkman often complained to my father about the treatment that he suffered, and even threatened to stop delivering milk. But when my father intervened, Lourdes worked herself into a fury: 'What now, sir, you listen to the milkman? Nothing, nothing, sir, he tells lies, sir. Look for yourself now. He puts cold water in the milk, sir. When I ask, he makes a monkey face, sir. How make *café au lait* with that?' She would turn to the milkman. 'Who and who milks the cow, now? Who? You? Your father?' she asked menacingly.

This daily scene left my father powerless. He watched the milkman walk towards the house of Monsieur Michel at the end of the street. He sat down, sighed and waited in the little thinnai for his newspaper. Every solution he hit upon had failed: having the milk delivered to Pattakka, who was one of the first in the neighbourhood to rise each morning; leaving the container near the door without waking anyone; asking my aunt to buy the milk. All useless.

The last shadows of Lourdes's morning dreams would vanish at the squawk of the pear-shaped horn the milkman attached to his handlebar.

Everything about him disgusted her: his way of looking at her, his snide and lecherous smile, his vulgar clothes. If not for the milk pot attached to his bicycle, no one would have taken him for a milkman. His flowery shirt and his 'Bobby' collar flapped in the wind like a dog's ears. His bellbottom pants were so tight at the waist that he had to adjust himself several times before mounting his bicycle. His father – if on some rare occasion he had to return to his old trade of delivering milk – came straight from the farm wearing a kaili and a piece of cloth slung on his bare chest. The son delivered milk as if he were going to a party. Nevertheless, he smelled like hay and cow farts.

With an apathetic gesture, he opened the lid of the old metal milk pot attached to the baggage rack of his shiny new bicycle, his pride. Three metal cups in different sizes hung from the edge of the baggage rack: 25cl, 50cl and one litre. He took the largest, showed Lourdes its bottom and dipped it into the milk pot, keeping his eyes on hers, a mocking smile curling the corners of his lips. Everyone knew, after all, about the different techniques that milkmen used to cheat you, such as putting a false bottom in their measures. Lourdes suspiciously followed the milkman's ambiguous gestures.

No sooner had the milkman left than Kaatannan's gaunt silhouette appeared. He sat down in the little thinnai and gave my father the newspapers. The two men had their daily ritual. They read the newspapers in silence, then talked politics as they enjoyed their coffee, listening to Lourdes rattle off the shopping to be done.

Lourdes was still angry when she brought the coffee. Kaatannan teased her, mocking her Creole accent: 'Who that there? How it go?' He regretted it immediately.

Lourdes clanged the silver cup down beside him. Drops of coffee scattered on the thinnai, spreading a delicious smell. Without speaking to Kaatannan, she said to my father, 'Monsieur, tell Brother Wind' – referring to Kaatannan – 'to buy roll rotis, sir. He never buy good bread.' Then she turned to face Kaatannan.

'From what baker you buy bread now? All soft, no taste. Buy from Grand Bakery. Much better. Same for steak, I say chewing gum. Who eat that? Someone with no teeth? If he can't, Monsieur, me I do shopping myself, Monsieur. He, he spends time talking with fish-women, flirting. Coming back always late. Sir says nothing, Monsieur's tricked. Brother Wind gets his crow.'

Like Lourdes, Kaatannan had been in our service for a long time. His family lived in the neighbourhood – on the other side of the little bridge by the stationery shop – but he had always lived with us. He did the shopping and other odd jobs. He and my father had met in school and became inseparable.

Kaatannan didn't care for Manickam Annan's reading sessions. He held that communists were utopian, power-mad agitators who spent their days conspiring. He made fun of Manickam's sign, which, according to him, depicted 'Mop head, Baldy and the Moustache'. In his opinion, before attacking the problems of the proletariat and the injustices of capitalism, the superstitions that had covered the land for thousands of years would have to be destroyed. India could throw off the European yoke and could write a new labour code, but it would never be free as long as caste hierarchy and religious hypocrisy reigned.

When they were young, Kaatannan and my father had been seduced by the message and the charisma of Periyar. They rallied to the Self-Respect Movement and threw themselves into the struggle for the rights of Dravidians. Armed with Tamil literature, they battled Brahminism. Until my father left for France, Kaatannan and he were ardent members of the Dravida Kazhagam Party that Periyar had founded. They shared his dream of a society without religion or caste. Animated by the fire of youth, exalted by the ideals of the party, the two friends went from one meeting to another. They protested in front of temples that refused access to Paraiyars. They helped inter-caste couples to wed, and widows to remarry.

My father left for France with sadness and hope. He was sad that he would not continue the struggle for his country's emancipation, but hopeful that the caste system – a social apartheid – would disappear. He was soon disillusioned. Not only did Periyar's party split, but the new parties that emerged from it – Dravida Munnetra Kazhagam and Anna Dravida Munnetra Kazhagam – were led by clowns and con artists who replaced the idols of Brahminism with the worship of themselves.

In spite of years of separation, the two men kept their friendship intact. When my father returned to Pondicherry after his military service, Kaatannan naturally came to work for us. He never seemed interested in starting his own family. Food, shelter and my father's friendship were enough for this smiling, carefree soul. He led a modest life and nurtured no ambitions. But there was one category of people Kaatannan couldn't tolerate: North Indians.

When we were still young enough for Kaatannan to walk with us to school, my brother and I suspected him of taking detours to avoid the ashram. He preferred walking the Cours Chabrol down to the Statue of the Unknown Soldier and then turning right on Rue Mahé de Labourdonnais, going as far as the hospital before turning on to Rue Victor Simonel, where our school stood. All this to avoid the ashram. If by some misfortune he crossed the path of an ashramite, he couldn't help muttering a famous line from one of MGR's films: 'Behold the treasure of my Dravidian-ness.' I never knew what that meant. I had never seen the film.

When we were younger, we loved to go to the market with Kaatannan, wandering down the narrow pathways – half in sun and half in shade – through the crowded streets. Kaatannan knew everybody; he stopped every hundred metres to say hello to someone. The bazaar had four entrances, but Kaatannan always took the one on Rue Gandhi. There was an entrance in front of the prison on Rue Dupleix, opening on the vegetable stands; another on Rue Bharati, for the florists; the third was on Rue Rangapillai, in front of the prosperous house of Dupleix's old courtier. Kaatannan's entrance was the loudest and most crowded – it was the entrance for the fish-women.

Lourdes's accusations were not unfounded. Kaatannan flirted with the fish-women, indifferent to the stink of fish. Sitting on their *manakatai*s, their saris lifted to their knees, armed with a knife and an *arivalmanai*, they shouted, waved their hands, argued and bargained. From time to time, they readjusted their saris and shot seductive glances at the men. The latter didn't stop for the best fish, they stopped for the best fish-woman. Each had her usual customers. If by some accident one of these customers took his business to another vendor because she had better fish, her stand would be transformed into a boxing ring. Garlands of curses would fly from the women's mouths; the fish would soon be ruined. The men watched the fist fights, enjoying themselves.

Kaatannan wandered happily among the fish stalls, stopping in front of some and chatting with their proprietors. But when we were with him, he didn't stay long. This was the only row of shops where we walked ahead of him. Pinching our noses, my brother and I hurried through it, careful not to brush against a shark's tail or a tuna dangling on the small counters. While Kaatannan stopped to flirt or buy fish, we headed to the row of spice shops on the left of the main entrance. We started sneezing as soon as we took our fingers off our noses.

Our favourite part was when Kaatannan would take us to the butchers. Their stalls ran along the last two rows in the far south of the bazaar. The sale of fish was a woman's work, but here was the kingdom of mighty, muscular men. The second-to-last row was for poultry. It stank of chicken, duck and turkey droppings. Feathers stuck to your skin as you walked through it, and it was just as noisy as the fish-women's area. There the women shouted, here it was the chickens that cackled along with the brusque quacks of ducks and the burbled gobbling of turkeys.

Kaatannan could spend hours in these two rows of shops. He would stop, inspecting the chickens from afar, then slowly approach the stand where they peeked their heads out of baskets. He would bend down in front of the merchant and begin discussing the chickens' merits. Once he was properly assured about the quality of their food and their place of origin, he would pick up two or three of them, initiating a session of measurement and observation. Holding a chicken by its feet, he would close his eyes and calculate how much it was worth as it writhed and screeched. If he was satisfied, he would call us over and explain the method of choosing a good chicken: the bird shouldn't be lying down or limp; its eyes should be dry, and its feathers, too; its feet should be smooth.

After this meticulous examination, negotiations began.

They could take half an hour or more. There were several steps. Kaatannan announced his price. Most of the time, the merchant didn't accept it, but tried to keep his customer. Kaatannan pretended to lose interest and continued shopping elsewhere. After some minutes, he returned to the row of shops, avoiding eye contact with the merchant. He started conversations with the seller's rivals, watching his target from the corner of his eye. Once he sighted a gesture of surrender, Kaatannan returned to the merchant, ready to finish the deal. The tired vendor nodded, pushing the chicken into Kaatannan's hands. The bird squawked and struggled between the two men, as its fate swung between life and death. Kaatannan always won. A huge grin appeared on his bony face as the merchant snatched a few moist and dirty rupee notes from his hand.

The atmosphere of the meat shops was different. Here, nobody shouted, argued or even bargained. Who would dare to raise their voice to the butchers, with their bulging muscles, bloody aprons and brutal faces framed by horseshoe-shaped moustaches? Here, everything was intimidating: the size of the men who worked their knives and spoke with booming voices; their gestures, which held so much violence; the hanging carcasses and carved portions of beef and mutton that dripped blood on the dirty tile floor. The butchers who weren't busy carving and slicing paced up and down the row, smoking cigarettes and kicking dogs that searched for fallen morsels.

Thursdays and Sundays were the liveliest parts of the week. Early in the morning, the boys would invade the butchers' row, elbowing each other and competing to buy the best meats before the soldiers arrived. With straw hats fastened on their heads, the soldiers strolled down the row with obvious contempt and nonchalance. They never bargained. They simply pointed gold-ringed fingers towards the finest cuts of meat, which had been reserved for them. Their expert eyes, hidden behind their Ray-Bans, scanned the cuts. From time to time, they fanned themselves with their straw hats, chasing away the flies that buzzed in this narrow passage where the smell of blood and flesh mingled with that of cologne from Colombani. The butchers dropped their usual aggression and put on their finest smiles.

Over the noise of knives, bits of conversation could be heard.

'So Pays,' one of the soldiers would ask another, 'what's cooking today?'

'Oh, the missus told me to buy mutton so she could make a korma. But I want a good steak with green pepper. Maybe I'll get both. She'll henpeck a little, but I'm used to that!' the other would reply with a wink.

'And yourself, Pays?'

'I just bought some beef fillets and now I'm going to the Vietnamese shop for some rice cakes and nuoc mam. Vietnamese on Sunday is a sacred rite for the missus. Weekdays are one thing, but on Sunday she has to have food from her country.'

'We'll meet afterward for an *apéro*?'

'Of course, where?'

'Liberty? Qualithé? Bar Américain? The Continental?'

'Let's do the Continental. It seems they have a new Sinhalese chef who works wonders. And I prefer drinking my *pastis* facing the sea; it reminds me of *La Canebière*.'

Then, the little group of soldiers, satisfied with their purchases, would disperse.

Kaatannan also had his favourite butchers. When mutton was the order of the day, he went to the stand of Anwar, a huge Muslim with a thick beard reddened with henna. He spent more time with his *misbaha* than his knife. He didn't need to shout or wave his arms to attract customers. His eyes half closed, he stood serenely by the counter. Kaatannan greeted him, 'Salam Alekum, Anwar Bhai!' The butcher returned his greeting, putting his right hand over his heart. 'Alekum Salam, Khaatu Bhai!' Kaatannan never negotiated with Anwar; he appreciated the Muslim's honesty and knew that he always had good meat.

But when it came to beef Kaatannan could be stubborn and unpleasant. He took his time studying, bargaining and arguing with the butcher, until the latter finally lost patience and surrendered to Kaatannan's whims. He only liked beef from the slaughterhouse of Oulgaret. Surrounded by rice fields and open spaces for grazing, this village was a perfect spot for raising cattle. Its beef was prized by connoisseurs, Kaatannan among them. Like an inspector sent on a mission by an imaginary bureaucracy, he would survey every inch of the shop, eyeing the cuts of beef suspiciously. Anxious and exasperated, the butcher would accept his price, happy to see him leave.

'Amma! Amma!' A voice calling from outside broke our concentration. My brother and I had been watching Selvanadin's father finish the last steps of his cooking. He was in the middle of carving the meat for the civet, placing it in a porcelain dish.

'Amma! Amma!' The voice was growing closer and more urgent. Lourdes turned to us. 'So go now! Go see who's calling. Maybe it's that beggar.'

Already angry that he had been waiting so long for his dinner, my brother ignored her. I had no choice but to get up and head towards the door myself.

'Thambi, can you please give me a glass of water? It's for my thaata,' the young man asked me with an embarrassed look. He apologized for disturbing me. Without a word, I took the cup and went to the kitchen, where there was a large vessel filled with water.

'Who is it now?' Lourdes asked me as she oversaw Selvanadin's father's work, keeping her eyes fixed on him.

'It's that old man. He wants some water.'

'But it's not him who called?'

'No, it's the boy,' I said, dipping the cup into the vessel.

'Careful!' Lourdes grabbed my arm. 'What a pig now! Look at this tumbler now – so dirty; you put that in the water? All dirty too! Now, now, you sit. Me, I give the water myself,' she said with annoyance. 'And first who is this boy?'

'I don't know! Go ask him yourself!' I answered, infuriated at being called a pig. My brother was bent over with laughter, which made me even angrier. I went to sit down further away, under the tree where a table and chairs had been set up for my uncle and his friends.

I saw them coming as Lourdes went to fetch the water. They looked pretty tipsy. They laughed and joked, and bottles clanked in their bags. They took off their shoes in the doorway, making sure to line them up carefully – because if there was one thing that could drive my aunt into a fury, it was shoes piled up by the door.

She didn't like her husband's friends. She thought that they were bumpkins who were ready to brawl after a few drinks – and that they exploited my uncle's generosity. Every week she had to buy kilos and kilos of meat, and have it cooked just to their tastes without them contributing anything.

Seated in the chairs beneath the naga tree, they would give Lourdes orders to bring them this and that. 'Serve me some more sauce. Give that box of matches. Get us some cigarettes.' All this without budging from their seats. They would toss cigarette butts on the ground, scatter bones all around them, belch, cough, hack and spit under the chairs and wipe their fingers on the garden plants. After they left, our courtyard always looked like a battlefield.

My uncle stopped Lourdes on her way out.

'Where are you headed, Lourdes? Get us some glasses and serve us a bit of vindail.'

'Wait, pa. I take water to that old man in the thinnai, then I come serve you.'

'Now that you mention it, who are those two in the thinnai?'

'I don't know, pa. They just came. The old man looked so tired and...now, that's strange. He didn't ask permission.'

'That's okay, Lourdes. He's an old man, he can rest wherever he wants. Go to him and come back quick.'

She came back after giving the dented cup to the boy who was waiting by the door, staring into the house and drooling with hunger.

5

My father arrived as Lourdes was finishing setting the table. He leaned his bicycle against the little thinnai and stopped at the doorway to observe the two strangers. By reflex, he nodded at the old man. Serving himself a glass of arrack, the latter returned his greeting. 'Hello sir. I wish you a happy Bastille Day.'

'Hello!' responded my father, unsurprised that the old man was speaking French.

'You must excuse us for sitting here, sir. I was so tired that I couldn't keep from taking shelter in your thinnai. It looked so comfortable. I wanted to sit here just long enough for my grandson to find me something to drink. It's so hot! And I heard that the liquor store was quite far. Please be kind. Let us rest here a few minutes. We'll leave just as soon as I can get back on my feet.'

My father looked at the glass that the old man had just set down beside him and answered with a smile, 'I don't see any problem with that, dear sir. Rest as long as you like. That's what the thinnai is for – to welcome visitors. There's no trouble. But, tell me, what's a man like you doing in this neighbourhood?'

'To tell the truth, sir, we were headed towards the liquor shop when I smelled your fine cooking...' Gilbert Thaata answered with a wicked grin. 'And I was so tired that Little Gilbert here said I should rest while he looked for something to celebrate this holiday. I must say that it made me so happy to set foot here in your house. Your servant and your children are so kind. Your sons are very handsome and polite, sir.'

The old man had found the password, and my father's face broke into a proud smile.

'There now, old one, you rest up and don't you hesitate if you need anything at all.'

'Thank you, thank you, good sir. I thank you from the bottom of my heart. Hey Gilbert! Thank the nice man!' he hissed, striking the boy with his elbow. Little Gilbert muttered an unintelligible thanks.

As he was about to step into the house, my father briefly hesitated. He thought he noticed the same sad expression on both faces. He turned to have a better look and saw two tragic faces unable to disguise their disappointment. He remembered that the old man had mentioned food. He stopped in the doorway, took off his shoes and spoke again.

'Wait here, old one, I'll be back in a few minutes.' He passed by the table, making sure that everything was in order, and continued to the kitchen. He called Lourdes, who was busy washing dishes, and told her to serve two plates of civet, chicken and French fries. Then he took a bottle of whisky from the sideboard. As he turned around, he was face to face with Lourdes. With her hands on her hips, she stared wrathfully at my father.

'Oh no, Monsieur, I won't give our *vasis* and glasses to those two now. They're not clean!'

My father furrowed his brows. What did she mean – was it the visitors or the glasses that weren't clean?

He was used to this kind of reaction from her. He usually smiled and let her do as she pleased. But that day when he saw her taking out two aluminium plates as dirty and dented as the old man's cup, he exploded.

'That's going too far, Lourdes! You're not going to serve good food in dishes like that? They can use ours – and keep them, if they want. Whoever drank whisky in an aluminium cup?' My father stalked off towards the thinnai with two glasses and the whisky. He sat down and opened the bottle.

'Surely you're not going to drink *sarayam* on Bastille Day. A good whisky will do you good, old one.' Gilbert Thaata, who had been slumping over like a cow in pasture, suddenly straightened up, his eyes shining at the sight of the bottle. He moved towards the edge of the thinnai.

'How do you take your whisky? Straight or with soda?' My father's question surprised the old man, who stared at the glass held out to him.

'I don't remember, dear sir! It's been so long since I've had any.' The old man took the glass with trembling hands. 'I would certainly like to take it straight, but if it's too strong, I'd have it with soda.'

My father turned to Little Gilbert and asked him to get some bottles of soda from Karika Bhai. The boy hesitated.

'You don't need any money. Tell him it's for the soldier. And get yourself something to drink, too.'

Meanwhile, Lourdes had prepared two plates of food. She set them in the thinnai beside the old man, whose face lit up. He closed his eyes and breathed in the smell.

'You are too kind, my dear sir! May God bless you and your family! You can't know how happy this makes me,' the old man stuttered. A tear had formed in his right eye, and began sliding down his dirty cheek.

Little Gilbert returned with two bottles of soda and a bottle of Limca. My father poured himself a little whisky, mixing it with soda. The old man waited for him to finish, then raised his glass and, in a broken voice, made a toast.

'To your health, sir! You honour me by sharing your meal with us. Gilbert and I would like to show you our gratitude, but we don't have anything. We're just two poor buggers fate has thrown into the street. May heaven bless you, and I thank God for leading us to you.'

'To your health, old one. You're welcome. It's a pleasure to have you with us for this holiday. *Tchin-tchin!*'

The old man held the glass with both hands. He brought it towards his lips and closed his eyes. His lips shook as he put them against the glass. He took a swig, grimaced and set the glass down on the floor of the thinnai. Turning to the plate of food, he looked for a fork. Not finding one, he stuck his hand into the civet. My father noticed this, and summoned Lourdes with an irritated voice.

She soon appeared. 'Yes, Monsieur?' Lourdes sometimes allowed herself to disobey my father, but she knew the signs of his anger. She was frightened. Her gaze shifted anxiously from the old man to my father, whose eyes flashed lightning.

'How do you think these men are going to eat? With their hands? Get the silverware.' His tone was brutal and imperious.

'But, Monsieur...'

Lourdes gave up trying to defend herself. She soon reappeared from the kitchen with the silverware, which she placed beside Gilbert Thaata.

'Oh sir, there was no need to go to this trouble. It's been so long since I've used a fork, and Gilbert doesn't even know how.' The old man flashed an apologetic expression at Lourdes.

'No, no, just because you're sitting in this thinnai doesn't mean you should be treated like a beggar,' my father insisted as he poured himself another drink.

Gilbert Thaata finished his whisky and was about to make short work of his meal.

'Wait, old one. We're just at the appetizer. I'll have you served some vindail with your whisky and then you can have your civet with a nice glass of wine.'

'Oh thank you, thank you, sir! You are so kind.'

It seemed that the old man hadn't received such gentle, generous treatment in many years. He mumbled into his beard and hardly dared to look my father in the eye. He was crushed under an avalanche of kindness. He didn't know whether to feel proud or humiliated: humiliated, because he was being treated like a beggar; or proud, because someone, finally, had recognized his true worth.

He emptied his glass, which my father promptly refilled, and plunged his fork into the vindail. He savoured his first bite with moans of pleasure. He moved his hand delicately, wielding the fork with a certain elegance. Pulling out a dirty handkerchief from his pocket, he wiped the corners of his mouth. He put the glass down beside him, took the plate of vindail in one hand and held the fork in the other.

The toenails sticking out from the holes in his shoes no longer made him feel ashamed. After his second glass, his clothes had become immaculate. Poverty and filth had disappeared. His back straight and head high, the old man began to act as if he were the special guest of some ambassador in the far-off embassy of our thinnai.

'So, how long have you been retired, sir? You seem awfully young to me.' His voice grew clearer and stronger.

My father was no great psychologist, but he knew human nature. He had pushed the two glasses of whisky on the old man knowing that they would give him confidence. My father was pleased at the transformation happening before him. He took out a packet of Charminar and offered the cigarettes to the old man.

'To be honest, sir, I prefer a *suruttu*,' the old man said, swallowing a piece of meat. He turned to Little Gilbert, who had just finished his meal. Hidden behind the old man, he had eaten in silence. He was now staring enviously at the old man's plate.

'Gilbert, go buy me a suruttu from the shop. You still have money, don't you?'

Watching Little Gilbert fumble despairingly in his pockets, my father told him to buy a suruttu from Karika Bhai and add it to the soldier's account, before answering the old man.

'Oh, I've been retired for twelve years now. I did the absolute minimum to earn my pension, and now I'm back.' He lit a cigarette.

'Why didn't you stay? You didn't like it in France?'

'It wasn't a question of liking it or not. I just wanted to come back to my own people. Even if I started a family there, it seemed natural to come back home.'

'But France, that's home too! You're a French citizen.'

My father exhaled a puff of smoke. He tapped the cigarette on the edge of the ashtray and seemed to think it over.

'Oh, I'm French. But Indian, too. I was born here. So were my ancestors. My roots are here. And after spending some time outside their own province, even a Breton or a Norman wants to go home. It's the same with me. But my home is a little further... You must know the history of Pondicherry as well as I do. My family has been French for generations, but I was the first one to go to France. Until then we were just paper Frenchmen; we were really Indians. And we still are. How can you feel French if you've never set foot there? My parents came from nothing; they didn't know the French language or culture. The only thing that connected us to the Europeans was the church. Besides that, it was two different worlds.'

'But all those years in the French army, didn't they make you feel like you were part of the nation?'

My father crushed his cigarette in the ashtray and poured another drink. He got up to fill the old man's glass and sat back down. He held his whisky in his right hand, watching the soda bubbles rise to the surface. He ran his left hand through his hair, which he always did when he had to think hard about something.

'I don't know your story, old one, but you seem like you know a thing or two about life. Living in exile is a curse. Sure, I chose it, but back then there wasn't much to choose from. Leaving was the only way out of poverty. Trenches, gunshots and rations – that was all we knew. We fought our brothers in Madagascar, Indochina and Algeria. We never thought we might be guilty of anything. We felt nothing, saw nothing, understood nothing. We fought the enemies of the motherland. We were proud. But in spite of our faithful service, we wanted to come home. We were just colonial soldiers. France was never our country. What we had with it was just a quirk of history.'

My father stopped a moment as he heard the noise of moving chairs. My brother and I had finished our meal. Lourdes cleared the table, shook the tablecloth and set new plates and silverware for my father. He stared intensely at the old man's face, wanting to continue speaking, but worried that he was keeping the man from his dinner.

My brother and I sat down beside our father on the thinnai. He rarely talked about military life. Sometimes, with his friends, he would dust off one or two memories, but he never spoke of them with us.

In contrast, the father of our classmate Paul loved telling stories about his military service. We pretended to believe in his implausible prowess. Paul would run off whenever these displays of mythomania started up; we'd catch him later and tease him.

His father's best story was about the time he was swallowed by a boa. As part of a secret and incredibly dangerous mission, Paul's father was driving an officer through the African bush. He got lost. After wandering for most of the night, they finally found the road. However, it immediately gave out in a cul-de-sac. They couldn't see anything ahead of them. And since it was a secret mission, the captain had ordered him to drive with the headlights off so that no enemies could spot them (Paul's father bragged that he could see in the dark as well as a cat). When he turned the jeep around, they were shocked to find that the road had been barred. They couldn't go back the way they had come.

They spent the night in the jeep. When they awoke it was still dark. They each took out a torch and observed that they seemed to be stuck in a tunnel with slimy walls. It didn't take long to figure out that they were in the belly of a snake. The captain fainted. But Paul's father, brave and cold-blooded himself, took his bayonet and cut his way out of the reptile while dragging the unconscious captain with one hand.

His stories had no limits, but he was invariably the hero. He caught bullets in the palm of his hand, slaughtered a thousand Viet Cong soldiers with a sweep of his machine gun and bombarded African villages from the air (although he wasn't a pilot). Even the scars from his childhood smallpox became war wounds.

'And that's why there's no French flag flying here?' the old man asked my father, who had sunk into his memories.

'In a way, yes. I never was much for patriotism. I don't feel the need to show my love for a country. My friends can feel it; they can put up a French flag in front of their houses, or the French and Indian flags together. I respect them. Personally, I don't feel it. I don't feel any pride either. The flag is just what the government uses to wrap corpses.'

I finally had the answer to a question that my brother and I had been asking each other for years. But, in fact, we did have a French flag. It was sleeping in the back of the chest of drawers, folded, dusty, waiting for its day. Just like the French citizenship papers.

'I understand better now, sir. I understand you, too,' the old man said as he finished his drink.

My father stood up and straightened his trousers. It was time to let the old man eat.

'You must be hungry, old one. *Bon appétit*. Lourdes will bring you a glass of wine. And, most importantly, get some rest. Have a nice nap, and you can leave whenever you want.'

'Thank you, good sir. I can never thank you enough for your generosity,' Gilbert Thaata said, trying to rise.

'It's nothing, old one.' My father put a hand on his shoulder, gesturing for him to stay seated. 'It was a pleasure to speak with you. It's not every day I meet someone who speaks French, especially in this neighbourhood.'

Once back inside the house, he opened a bottle of wine himself and handed Lourdes a glass to take to the old man. As she was about to head out to the thinnai, he gave her a straw mat. She looked at him with astonishment.

'Why this, Monsieur?'

'For the old man,' my father answered.

'But, Monsieur, he didn't even ask for it! You're too nice to him.'

'I didn't ask you, Lourdes. Take this to the gentleman and then serve me some vindail. It looks so good.'

Without acknowledging the compliment, Lourdes began to mutter, 'What's happened to Monsieur? Treating the old man like someone so important. He's not the king of Vattalakundu!'

A little disturbed by this conversation, my father headed towards the group sitting under the naga tree. He considered my uncle's friends worthless and normally avoided them. Their main activities were getting drunk and avoiding work. My father, a soldier and a Frenchman, had a certain standing, but the social circle of my uncle, a foreman at the Rodier factory, was proletarian and penniless. My father frequented the Cercle de Pondichéry, the Bar Américain, Hôtel d'Europe and Hotel Qualithé, while my uncle was usually seen in Sarayakadai No. 1 or Kallukadai No. 3.

It wasn't their financial situations that made the difference. My uncle had a good income and if he had wanted to he could have gone to the same establishments as my father. But he was a stranger in that bourgeois world. Material comfort seemed useless in his eyes. He never bothered furnishing the house. My aunt spent all her time taking care of her sick mother, leaving their house early and returning late at night. His only luxury was books. He and my father hadn't been able to continue their studies when they were young, but they still had a thirst for education. My uncle spent his days lying on a straw mat in the shade of the naga tree savouring the breeze that blew through its branches, newspapers and books scattered around him. It was the only place where the two men could be in perfect communion with each other.

My father kept his books on a massive bookshelf built of red-brown teak. It was his pride. The day he bought it, he rearranged the whole sitting room and made it the centre of the house. He replaced the dining table with a new one that matched the bookshelf. He repainted the wall behind it to make it seem more imposing. Whenever he acquired a new book, he would open the doors of the bookshelf as ceremoniously as a priest opening temple doors. He would slowly consider the best place for the newcomer, shifting the books with infinite patience, as if solving a puzzle.

For many years, my father kept the key to the bookshelf out of our reach. It hung beside the crucifix on the opposite wall. Books were sacred, too. Jesus, his head tilted to the right, looked despairingly at the key. But when we had grown up a little, the key found its rightful place in the keyhole of the holy bookshelf.

At first my brother and I hardly dared to touch it. We stared at each other and then at the little silver key that could open the door to the adult world. Just opening the doors and smelling the enigmatic odour of old books drowned me in bliss. I read the titles aloud: Nilakanta Sastri, *The History of Southern India: From Pre-History to the Fall of Vijayanagara*; *The Journal of Ananda Rangapillai*; Ambedkar, *Annihilation of Caste*. Shoulder to shoulder like silent knights guarding the fortress of knowledge, the books waited to do battle against my intelligence.

My father knew the language of Molière as well as that of Thiruvalluvar, but my uncle only knew Tamil. My father was French and my uncle was Indian. This anomaly was an inheritance of the colonial regime.

On 3 January 1882, my great-grandfather Nalanda presented himself at Pondicherry's newly built City Hall. He was tired from the journey on foot from Ariyankuppam, but impressed by the stately building in front of him. Hesitant and anxious, he got in line behind many other people waiting to make an important decision. Two hundred years ago, one of his ancestors had converted to Catholicism to escape untouchability. Now Nalanda was about to dive into another new world, seeking a better life for himself and his children. He would become a French citizen.

An escape route from poverty had opened on 21 September 1881, when the French government passed its law of 'renunciation'. The people waiting in line with Nalanda were excitedly discussing the issue while two groups outside the line shouted at them, trying to influence their decision. The first was the lawyer Ponnoutamby's clique; they encouraged renunciation. The second was the squadron of Chanemougam – the 'Black Louis XI', the Machiavellian – the opponent of renunciation.

The two men, in fact, were from the same caste of Vellalas. But Ponnoutamby belonged to the city Vellalas, who worked in the colonial administration. They had converted to Catholicism and believed in the values of the French Republic. Chanemougam was one of the rich landowners who reigned in the villages. He was the head of the traditionalist Hindus who opposed everything foreign. Ponnoutamby was the first Indian to 'renounce', taking the new name of La Porte. Chanemougam hated him.

Nalanda couldn't afford to fight for an ideology. He wanted to give his family a better future. He was ready. What was he giving up? A vile, shameful condition had been imposed on him. Would it be such a sacrifice to have a new name, one that didn't have any caste connotations? Didn't it make sense to pursue a better status, even if it was a foreign one? As he moved forward in the line, things gradually grew clearer. By the time he was facing the bureaucrat and the two witnesses, there was no shadow of a doubt. The devil take tradition!

On his way back, his steps were more assured. He felt lighter. Centuries of abjection and abomination had been erased by a bit of ink on his thumb. He couldn't stop marvelling at this magic; pushing his thumb on a sheet of paper had changed his destiny.

But destiny, and the French bureaucracy, had another round to play. In 1962, Charles de Gaulle ratified the secession of Pondicherry to the Republic of India. The ill-informed inhabitants reeled in panic. Those who had 'renounced' didn't understand why they needed to choose French nationality again. In spite of the confusion, some five thousand families managed to become French. The 'renouncers' who hadn't declared their desire for French citizenship became Indians. Thus it was hardly uncommon to see two nationalities rubbing uncomfortably against each other within the same family. That's what happened with my father and my uncle.

My father had joined Periyar's Self-Respect Movement when he was young, but my uncle, in contrast, was a communist. He was one of the first to follow V. Subbaiah when he created a union for textile workers and began publishing the pro-independence newspaper *Soundaridam*. According to my uncle, Periyar was just a self-important fool whose hatred of Brahmins had led him to negotiate with the British. Periyar had indeed told them that they could keep the Madras Presidency if they wished. No one, not even the British, had taken his offer seriously. Neither could my uncle stand the way Periyar mocked Tamils, saying Tamil was a barbarous language, and made himself, a Kannadiga, the head of the Dravidian movement, as if Tamils couldn't have done it themselves.

Everything separated my father and uncle. Their ideas, their politics, their friends, their lives. But mutual respect and brotherly love held them together.

6

The burning sun was vanishing behind the rice fields of Oulgaret when my brother and I were about to leave to join the evening's festivities. Lourdes waited for us with coffee and cakes; she passed us five ten-rupee notes that my father had given her for our expenses.

'Be careful now. So many people there! Many, many thieves.' Her warnings were lost amid the monstrous snoring that rose from the thinnai.

'Don't worry, Lourdes. We'll be careful. We're not babies.' My brother gave her his empty cup and stuffed the notes in his pocket.

'I know now. So you got big fast.' She walked with us to the door and cast a disgusted glance into the thinnai. Chubby flies buzzed above the plates, where bones and scraps were scattered. Empty glasses and dirty silverware lay on the ground. The wine glass had overturned, and beneath it a dark stain had grown on the dirt floor.

The old man snored. Amused passers-by stopped to listen. The thinnai seemed to be a cage in which wild beasts growled. A fat, hairy belly freckled with crumbs poked out of his dirty safari jacket, rising and falling as he breathed. In his intoxicated slumber, he muttered and ground his teeth. There was no trace of the boy who had been with him.

Lourdes let us go and picked up the dishes. She headed to the fountain to wash them, grumbling all the way. When she got there, she realized she was too early; the water wasn't running yet. She was just about to return home when she saw Little Gilbert and Three-Balls Six-Faces drinking tea on the bench.

'He didn't lose time, that one. Already he knows the worst person in the neighbourhood,' she muttered to herself as she stared at them. The two boys giggled and joked, their eyes fixed on the Killer Widow's house. Lourdes summoned Little Gilbert with a wrathful voice. He set his glass on the bench and sauntered towards her.

'Yes, Lourdes, what can I do for you?' he asked with a snide smile.

Lourdes stared at him, shocked, and then pulled herself together for a furious response.

'What now? So what are these manners now? First, you know my name? Don't wave your tail at me! Cut your tail off! Call me Lourdes one more time, beat you with the *sappath*, watch! Go, now, go! Fuck off and wake your grandfather.'

The young man stared at her. Scratching his head, he turned to Three-Balls Six-Faces, who was busy making obscene gestures at Lourdes. She flung the dishes to the ground, lashed Little Gilbert with a hateful look and took off for the house.

My brother and I headed towards the statue of Gandhi, where the last events of the holiday were taking place. On the way, we stopped at the home of my brother's classmate Alexis. He was showing off the gaudy medals that he'd won earlier that day. Like his soldier father, he had hung them on his right breast pocket, which sagged under the weight of his prizes.

In addition to his other faults of being a liar and an idiot, Alexis was possessed by an obsession with gambling.

When we passed the playing field of the ashram on the Cours Chabrol, Alexis flung himself into his favourite pleasure.

'The Tibetan'll win today, want to bet?' he asked my brother.

'Okay. Five rupees on the Indian.'

'Hm! No, not five rupees...here's what we'll do. If you lose, you give me five. If I lose I'll give you one of my medals. Look, this one here. I won it in the high jump.' He proudly pointed to a decoration made of brilliant yellow-coloured metal.

'You must think I'm an idiot, Alexis. Your medal's not worth one rupee. And it's ugly.'

'But the French consul gave it to me himself.'

'To hell with the consul,' my brother answered. 'Five rupees or nothing.'

Alexis seemed to hesitate. He looked doubtfully at his medal, disappointed that it had failed to impress my brother.

'Okay, no medal. But two rupees instead of five. Okay?'

'Okay, two rupees.'

We arrived at the boxing ring. We heard the waves crashing against the wall of the athletic centre. The boxing ring was closer to the street than to the sea, so we could watch the boxers through the holes in the wall. Alexis often came with us to watch them, but not because he enjoyed the show. He was there to bet. And last time, he had lost on the Tibetan. He wanted revenge.

He was crestfallen to find the ring empty. No shadow of a boxer, not even a pair of gloves hanging from the ropes. Alexis wiped the sweat beading on his downy moustache. The medals drooped towards the ground.

'What do we do now?' he asked, distraught. Now that they had fallen in the dirt, the medals looked like pieces of scrap metal.

'What do you mean, "what do we do?" – there's nothing to do. It'll have to be some other time.'

'No! Couldn't we wait a bit?'

'No way,' my brother answered. 'I don't want to miss them setting up the greased pole on account of a two-rupee bet.'

Giving no further attention to Alexis's disappointment, we continued on our way. Alexis pressed his face against the rough wall as he peered into the gym, hoping to catch sight of someone. There was only the guard, who slept with his mouth open in a corner of the ring as if he had been struck unconscious by an invisible boxer. Alexis gathered his dusty medals and caught up with us near the French consulate, where Dupleix's statue wore a severe expression as we passed.

'So we'll bet on the pole, then? My money's on Martial.'

'I'm not interested in your bet, Alexis. And everybody in Pondi knows Martial's going to win. It's no secret.'

Rickshawallas were dancing beneath the lighthouse to the beating of drums. The effects of their morning alcohol had hardly evaporated. Some had given themselves a fresh coat of paint, while others had no trace left of the French tricolour and looked like bees with a single red stripe still marking their black bodies. They buzzed about pathetically, begging for money.

Another group, the Milestones, had white stripes on their tired bodies. They leaned against the wall of the All India Radio building. Their broken bows lay beside conical multicoloured hats, the peaks of which had begun to droop. The exhausted men had been wandering the streets all day long. But as soon as they saw soldiers, they reached into their last reserves of strength and began a fevered dance.

Nobody knew the origin of this bizarre custom, this dance of rickshawallas dressed like hunters and painted in the colours of the tricolour flag. What were the bows and arrows supposed to represent? And the pointed hat? The only thing that seemed to mean anything was the French flag.

As they waited for the greased pole – the highlight of the evening – the crowd divided itself among various entertainments. Shouts arose from the field behind the All India Radio building, where the 'dance of the tiger' had begun. A man dressed as a tiger was just about to kill a miserable goat that ran about trying to hide among the spectators' legs. The tiger-man, quite drunk, licked his 'paws' and fired hungry glances at his prey. Intoxicated by the crowd's applause, the man worked himself up more and more, and suddenly leaped forward. The enraptured audience held their breath as they watched his body rise into the air...then their faces tightened into masks of pain. The tiger-man had crashed to earth, dislocating his neck. While the crowd drew closer to him, the goat capered joyfully beneath the statue of Nehru.

It was getting harder to move through the thickening crowd. People filled the little square where Gandhi's statue was surrounded by the columns of the Gingee Fort, going up and down the little steps that led to the sea. Children and adults were building sandcastles or playing among the waves. My brother and I decided to go in the opposite direction, where thousands had gathered around the street vendors near the aayi mandapam.

Carts full of apples, dates, mangoes and pears – especially pears, it was the season – were lined on both sides of the street. Balloon sellers wandered amidst the crowd, stopping in front of crying children who grabbed their parents' clothes as they begged them to buy one of the yellow and red apple-shaped balloons. Seated on the ground, other vendors sold little items made of clay. Kitschy-coloured, clumsily made statuettes stood in file on pieces of cloth. Little clay drums covered in suspicious-looking leather emanated strange odours and sold like hot cakes. Their ear-numbing din added to the varied noises of the crowd.

Children played in Raj Nivas park, screaming as their parents looked on calmly while munching fried peanuts, spicy chickpeas and pieces of green mango from rolled-up newspaper cones. After their snacks were finished, some of them became engrossed in reading the papers while their kids splashed in the fountain, climbed trees and played on the slide in front of Hotel Qualithé. Some rolled down a little hill, on the top of which a cluster of hippies were gathered. The older boys tried to force open the old wooden door under the slide to access the legendary underground passage from Pondicherry to Gingee Fort.

The hippies, clutching their guitars, hardly noticed the hullabaloo around them. Seated in a circle beneath the only tree on the hill, they felt detached from everything. This was their holy mountain. Even the police, after making a few initial arrests, had decided to leave them alone. Parents and officials were baffled by this new phenomenon. Hidden by ganja smoke and armed with chillums, Pondicherry's youth were leading their own revolution.

Five hundred years ago, Kaduveli Siddhar, who lived in the village of Irumbai, had plunged into a deep and powerful meditation while sitting beneath an enormous peepal. The energy radiating from his body was so intense that the little kingdom of Edayanchavadi was struck with drought. The rivers vanished and the once fertile soil became dry red clay. Everyone was suffering, but no one dared to disturb the Siddhar's meditation and risk his curse. The king of the little kingdom didn't know what to do. He summoned the people. No one could think of a solution, until a devadasi named Valli told the king that she could pry the holy man away from his meditation.

The Siddhar was subsisting on peepal leaves, which he gathered without opening his eyes. He just spread his arms and the leaves fell right into his palms. Knowing this, Valli made *appalam*s as fine and light as the leaves themselves, and began to drop them in the Siddhar's hands day after day. He had been practising severe austerities for such a long time that he soon began to appreciate this new food – and the beautiful woman who provided it.

His appetite reawakened and his meditation ceased. An abundant rain covered the land; the people of Edayanchavadi were flooded with joy.

To thank Valli, the king hosted a huge feast in Irumbai's thousand-year-old temple. Valli herself was to dance there, in front of a lingam that Makaalar rishi had erected. When the night of the festival came, the temple was full of people. The king was there to watch the dance, and the Siddhar was the guest of honour.

Drunk on her success and the applause of the spectators, Valli began to dance so wildly that she lost her *salangai*, which threw her off balance. The holy man, full of compassion, picked up the anklet and returned it to Valli's ankle.

This act stupefied the crowd. The king and priests were horrified. How could such an honourable holy man touch the feet of a prostitute? The crowd began to gossip and joke, much to Kaduveli Siddhar's annoyance. He prayed for a rain of stones to prove his innocence. And immediately a great hail fell from heaven, smashing the lingam into countless pieces.

The Siddhar dealt them a terrible curse: wherever the stones were scattered, a terrible drought, more terrible than any before, would strike. The king and the crowd were terrified, and begged forgiveness from the holy man. Once the latter had calmed himself, he told them that his curse was irrevocable. The drought, however, would end on the day when strangers from far away came to live there, bringing fertility back to the earth.

In 1968, when Auroville was created, the horrified people of Pondicherry witnessed the arrival of a horde of strangers: dirty, bearded, long-haired, shabby and barefoot. They wandered the city shirtless in unkempt kailis that showed their skinny legs as Pondicherrians looked on in disgust. Those who were accustomed to the well-dressed Europeans frequenting private clubs and the Cercle de Pondichéry were shocked by these hippies meditating naked on the beach. The veterans who had fought in Indochina, Algeria and in other dirty wars of *la nation* could only listen in bafflement to these drugged-up messiahs preach peace on earth. How could they understand this generation of lost children who had thrown themselves out on the roads of Asia in search of spiritual wisdom? Kaduveli Siddhar must have laughed.

At first Pondicherrians, too, simply mocked the strangers. But when their own children started imitating these white sadhus, they sounded the alarm. But they hardly needed to have worried. Their children only shared a taste for daydreams and drugs; they had no interest in the hippie fakirs' spiritual quest, in these new-age gurus who lived in an illusory city of utopian dreams.

The Pondicherrian hippies were children of soldiers and middle-class families, students of the Collège Français, Collège Calvet or Tagore Arts College. They just wanted to be in fashion. They would rather talk about Sartre, Krishnamurthi, Che Guevara and the Vietnam War than mysticism. Their bearded, sad-eyed faces seemed angelic to Pondicherrian girls, who fell in love with the gentle dreamers in their flowery shirts and bell-bottomed jeans as the clacking of their wooden sandals echoed from dusk till dawn. The town's barbers and tailors could only look on sadly.

Drugs invaded Pondicherry. Young hippies strolled through the park, along the beach and in the botanical gardens with their heads befogged by every drug the world offered. Pondicherry was an artificial paradise, where you could find Manali charas, grass from Idukki, Bombay Black, Calcutta opium, bhang from Orissa, Kodaikanal mushrooms and *datura* from the outskirts of town.

Young people lived in a cloud of fantasies. Many died. Every week there was news that so-and-so had fallen from a tree trying to pick the moon like a fruit or drowned trying to swim with his brothers the fish.

Since the greased pole contest had not yet begun, we went off to quench our thirst at Mani's famous sherbet stand in front of UCO Bank. As I sat on a tiny stool, my mind began meandering through memories. Each neighbourhood had its own benevolent association that would parade in front of the French consulate and the governor's villa on the day of the festivities. Boulevard Nord had the 'Morning Star', Boulevard Sud had the 'Friendly Nest' and the central boulevard had the 'Social Awakening'. All of these associations gathered boys together in distinctive uniforms and under their particular flag. Preparations for the parade began months in advance. Children from the neighbourhood would practise marching under the severe gaze of an old soldier, who for some weeks would release all the frustration and humiliation that he himself had suffered in his service to the flag. And besides the parade, there were all sorts of Bastille Day games for which they had to train.

My brother and I would watch, full of jealousy, the Morning Star boys practise along Boulevard Nord. I wanted so badly to carry the big star made of transparent paper with a light bulb inside it that cast an image of a man showing off his muscles. I wanted to practise running like they did, holding eggs in spoons in their mouths, or try the sack race. I would watch the boys trying to climb the greased pole to the sausages, hams and other prizes on top. But what I wanted most was to catch the ducks that were thrown into the sea.

No, my brother and I couldn't be a part of any of it; we were told that we were too young. But that wasn't true. After all, Paul, Edouard, Alexis and other boys our age, schoolmates of ours, also took part. We couldn't participate for the same reason that we couldn't have a French flag flying above our home.

My father had a different way of spoiling us. He would take us on the eve of Bastille Day to the torchlit vigil at the *Foyer du Soldat*. After the vigil, he would take us to the Cercle de Pondichéry. While he talked with his friends, we would play all kinds of games around the tennis court and in many rooms of the club until late in the evening. We ate and drank everything we could. On the way back, my father would stop at Maleappa's butcher shop on the corner of Rue François Martin and Rue Desbassyns de Richemont. We would walk home with our arms full of treasures.

On 14 July, after the parade and the games, my father would take us to Gandhi's statue for the duck chase – the key moment of the first part of the day. The bravest boys gathered behind the statue, waiting impatiently. Others, sitting on the rocks, watched with melancholic eyes and passed the chillum. The participants couldn't enter the water before the ducks did, and the signal to begin was only given once the birds were a good distance from the shore. Then, at the sound of a whistle, the boys leapt in. To shouts of encouragement and applause, dozens of boys struggled in the sea and returned triumphant, clutching exhausted ducks by the neck.

After the chase, my father would carefully avoid the other soldiers who gathered by the Statue of the Unknown Soldier for souvenir photos. How I wished that my father would be with the soldiers whose chests were hung with medals shining in the July sun. He preferred to disappear in the crowd. He would wave to some people he knew as he slowly walked us towards the corner of the park, where he had left his bicycle under the eye of Mani the sherbet vendor. He'd buy us lemon sherbet before we left.

My father would take us past Liberty Hotel that stood on the road to Uppalam beside a field that the French army had used for target practice. He told us that this was where V.V.S. Aiyar had perfected Vanchinathan's aim before the latter assassinated Ashe, collector of Tirunelveli. Sitting on the steps of the little platform, my father would recount the daring exploits of the heroes of the independence movement.

We heard how Aiyar had left London, where he had been a lawyer, and fled Paris, where he had been accused of leading an anarchist conspiracy. His escape from Paris to Pondicherry disguised as a Muslim struck us with wonder. When he arrived in Pondicherry, in league with other independence activists, he became Vanchinattan's mentor, training him to use a revolver right here on this very ground. Ashe was assassinated at the Maniyachi station, and Vanchinattan killed himself to escape arrest. V.V.S. Aiyar drowned a few years later, trying to save his daughter.

My father would find a few of his friends at the Liberty Bar. Like him, they dressed in simple clothes, with no medals or other signs of belonging to the special caste of soldiers. While the adults drank their aperitifs, we'd go off to play. Sometimes we would look for fish in the wells at the far end of the field, near the salt marsh. We watched dark, tired shadows marching up and down the white pyramids of salt.

As evening came, we would watch the last games held on the Gandhi Tidal as we waited eagerly for the fireworks.

When it was over, my father brought home two tired boys who had fallen asleep to the lullaby of the squeaky bicycle chain, their dreaming heads full of sounds and colourful explosions.

But all of that was in the past. I already missed my childhood – and I had been in such a hurry to grow up!

Things had changed. I no longer went to the Bastille Day festival holding my father's hand. The games that we played were over. The meats of Maleappa's butcher shop and Liberty Hotel had disappeared. Time had already wiped away one era of my life.

7

'My family was struck with the curse of Sita.' Gilbert Thaata started his story in a tragic tone. He had had his first glass of whisky and was clutching the second, which my father had just served him, with a trembling hands. He lit a suruttu and took a long drag. His memories drifted behind the smoke that rose into the starry night.

Gilbert Thaata and his protégé had been living in our thinnai for some time now. The old man was an unapologetic do-nothing. His days consisted of sleeping, eating and drinking. He seemed to be the victim of a pathological immobility, only stirring to give orders to Little Gilbert or to frighten the neighbourhood children. Their parents would tell them: 'If you don't eat, I'll give you to Vellakarai Thaata. He'll put you in his sack and take you back to his country.' Children were afraid to leave their houses. The old man joined in the game. This earned him the sympathy of the parents, who at first had been afraid of him themselves.

Gilbert Thaata, in spite of his poverty, was a white man. Three centuries of French rule had left its marks on the collective psyche. A filthy, penniless Durai was still a Durai. But Gilbert Thaata's shaggy hair and dirty clothes didn't keep the people of the neighbourhood from paying him exaggerated respect. While they usually rushed newcomers, pressing them for their stories, they were reserved with Gilbert Thaata. You couldn't treat a European like an Indian. Gradually the old man acquired a status in the neighbourhood. He was like a pasha in his squalid kingdom. Pascal Pig-Tail brought him boudins. Velankanni brought made him special fish sauces. Asamandi Baiyacaca Sonal shared his bottle.

The neighbourhood had adopted the old man and Little Gilbert.

In the meantime, Manickam Annan's office had become the headquarters of the local Communist Party. Monsieur Michel was beside himself now that the neighbours all called Manickam Annan 'Monsieur' too. When Michel learned that Manickam Annan was planning to run for election for the post of naattamai, he nearly had a heart attack. Even if he didn't see any importance in such a title, the idea that Manickam Annan was becoming someone important enraged him. He was afraid that Manickam Annan's ambitions might run contrary to his own affairs. Manickam Annan might slow his own climb to the top – or even halt it.

After all, the Communist Party was opposed to the ashram and its newcomers. It resisted Sri Aurobindo's transformation into a spiritual idol and the Sanskritization of the local linguistic heritage. It saw the ashram's success as a new northern power-grab in Tamil country. But these spiritual immigrants formed the most important part of Monsieur Michel's customer base.

From Bengal, Orissa, Gujarat and Bihar, hundreds came to Pondicherry in pursuit of their master's sadhana. Some searched for Aurobindo's 'superior man' in Auroville, which had only just been built. Their quest for the 'super-mental' ended in the red dirt of Kuyilappalayam. The town was more like an anarchist kibbutz than the Vedic ashram they had imagined. The little villages past Boulevard Nord, once inhabited by fishermen and untouchables, were now about to become part of an ashramite zone. The miserable old shacks were making way for new houses and apartments, white-and-grey structures with names like 'Shanti', 'Aurore', 'Blessing' and 'Atma'.

Monsieur Michel swelled his wealth with these transactions. He convinced poor buggers to sell their land for a pittance, then resold it to the newcomers for a fat profit. Hungry for money and power, he thought up new professions for himself. From 'real estate developer', he had become 'architect', 'foreman' and even 'engineer'.

Also, Ramu had opened a bicycle repair shop beside his tea shop. His layabout brother Kanda spent his time pretending to tinker with worn-out bicycles. Imprisoned among greasy chains and exploded tyres, he pined for Suguna, the Killer Widow's sister. The boy's lovesick stares exasperated Ramu, who shot him hateful glances as he served tea.

My father came home unusually early that night. Gilbert Thaata sat in the thinnai, listening to Asamandi Baiyacaca Sonal's thousandth version of the Ethiopian Campaign. The old man looked annoyed. He hardly listened as he worried about tomorrow. He was out of money. He wondered how he would manage to live out the last days of his long and burdensome existence. He puffed at his last suruttu. The bottle he had shared with Asamandi Baiyacaca Sonal was empty. A few drops of sarayam stained the floor.

Gilbert Thaata listened to the old soldier's endless adventures with his eyes half closed. He was tired, but his spirit couldn't rest without its ration of alcohol.

His face lit up when he saw my father.

'You've come home early tonight, Monsieur,' he said with ostentatious politeness as he turned away from Asamandi Baiyacaca Sonal.

'Yes, I was feeling a bit tired and I wasn't in the mood to go to the Cercle tonight.' My father lit a cigarette and looked jovially at the two old men. 'So what's Asamandi Baiyacaca Sonal saying?'

'Oh, him! Monsieur, it's always the same story. Libya, Syria, Lebanon, Ethiopia. I've heard it so many times I feel like I've been to those faraway countries myself. But you know, the poor man, he has no one to talk to. His koratti, who has never set foot out of Mailam, won't understand a word about all those African countries. So we keep each other company,' the old man replied. His last words rang with sadness. My father noticed.

Gilbert Thaata put the burned-out suruttu to his lips and tried to inhale. Irritated, he stared at the wet chunk in his fingers and flicked it against the floor of the thinnai. The little oil lamp cast its shadow on the wall. It flickered in the faltering light.

Old Asamandi Baiyacaca Sonal finished his story. It seemed like he was waking up from a long nap. His bleary gaze wandered from my father to Gilbert Thaata. He wanted to rise, but his legs refused. Putting a hand on Gilbert Thaata's shoulder, he propped the other against the thinnai wall and called for his third wife, the koratti, whose name no one knew. She came as soon as she heard him calling. She took him by the arm and led him home.

As soon as he was gone, Gilbert Thaata put his empty bottle back into his sack. The empty glass taunted him. His glance fell on the glass of the old soldier, which still had a bit of sarayam. He wanted to take it. If he had been alone, he wouldn't have hesitated. But he pretended not to see it, and looked at my father. His blue eyes expressed his helplessness. He smiled awkwardly and my father disappeared without saying a word. Gilbert Thaata was uneasy. My father returned a few minutes later with a bottle of Bagpiper and a glass.

'Do you want to drink a bit with me, old-timer?' He opened the bottle and poured himself a drink.

The old man leapt to his feet. 'Of course, Monsieur! It would be a great pleasure,' the old man stammered. He sat on the edge of the thinnai and moved the glass towards my father.

'My family was struck with an Indian curse. The story goes back a long way...' Gilbert Thaata had hardly started before his voice was drowned out by the roar of a crowd. Three-Balls Six-Faces was acting out a movie he had seen that afternoon at the Ambika theatre. My father took advantage of the interruption to give an order to Lourdes.

'Lourdes, go get some suruttus for Gilbert Thaata.'

'And why myself, Monsieur? What nerve now! Send Fat Gilbert, him, he's got nothing to do.' Lourdes pouted, moving her mouth side to side. She stepped out into the street and called the boy. Little Gilbert was lying on the ground receiving kicks from Three-Balls Six-Faces. Three-Balls Six-Faces had made him run through the coconut grove to re-enact the last scene of the film: MGR pursuing Nambiar in a Buddhist temple in Bangkok. Gilbert Nambiar escaped the clutches of MGR Three-Balls Six-Faces and headed towards the thinnai, brushing the dust from his clothes.

Every evening as darkness fell, the neighbours would gather beneath a street lamp to watch the show by Three-Balls Six-Faces. He could recreate a whole film by himself. He could imitate the hero, the villain, the comic relief, the heroine and all the minor parts. His ability to change his voice to fit the character delighted everyone. He could sing and dance, do comedy and tragedy. His dramatic scenes made women weep. But his favourites – and those of the neighbourhood children – were the action scenes. His hands could transubstantiate any trifle. A stick between his legs became a stallion and in his hands, a rifle against imaginary foes. The handle of an old umbrella became a fearsome sword capable of piercing right through whichever member of his audience was filling in for the villain. This was the only moment of the day when the obtuse young man, usually the object of neighbourhood scorn, became a hero acclaimed by its inhabitants. Little Gilbert's providential arrival had added immensely to his happiness. The newcomer became his heroine, villain, comic relief...in a word, his whipping boy.

'Hey, Fat Gilbert, go get suruttus for Grandpa.' She shot him a look full of disgust, then returned to the kitchen. She came back a few minutes later with a plate of grilled meat, which my father loved to eat with his aperitif. She put a stool in front of my father, and set the plate on it.

'Give me your plate, Grandpa. I'll get you some *varutta cari*, too.' Lourdes knew how it was now. She didn't try to oppose my father when he sat out drinking with Gilbert Thaata. She reappeared with the old man's plate, set it on the edge of the thinnai and sat by the door.

'I was saying that my family was struck with Sita's curse,' Gilbert Thaata started again, taking a small drag on his cigar.

'The story goes far back, to about the seventeenth century. My ancestors came from the north of France. Well, to say it plainly, they were simple people, peasants from a little village near Douai. They lived on their land with their worries and their pains. Douai was fought over by the Flemish, the Spanish and the French. Around 1595, the French burned the village. All the houses were destroyed. One of my ancestors – his name was Mathurin Picav – had the wild idea of starting his life again, of going on an adventure. This peasant had never left home, but he decided he would make his fortune at the other end of the world.

'The young Mathurin Picav said goodbye to his family and embarked on a ship, the *Hammer*, under the command of Captain François Grout. It was accompanied by another, the *Crescent*. There were two adventurers whose names will reappear in this story: François Martin and Pyrard de Laval. Now, Mathurin, he had never travelled by sea before, the poor man! But he could tell right from the start that this would be no easy voyage...'

The journey began with forebodings. The *Hammer* had only sailed for a few leagues when its foremast snapped. Carpenters from the two ships hurriedly repaired it as the crew watched on, discouraged and suspicious. They already regretted setting sail.

Unpleasant surprises continued. On the 21st of May, at dawn, the *Hammer*'s sails were punctured by a cannonball. Startled awake, the crew rushed to prepare for battle. The captain ordered them to fire twice on the fleet of nine Dutch ships that were moving towards them. Stunned that his enemies did nothing in response to his counterattack, he was relieved to learn that the gunner of the Dutch vice admiral, drunk on *brandewijn*, had simply botched an attempt to fire in the air as a sign of respect to the French vessel.

As the weeks went on, the ships continued their route to Madagascar. There they were caught in an enormous storm. The ships were badly damaged and unable to continue without repairs. This delay proved deadly; heat and illness killed forty men. The captain, however, was not discouraged. The voyage would continue, until the end.

On the night of 2 July, the crew was woken by shouts and groans. A violent shock rattled the vessel. Captain Grout had been lying sleepless in bed, thinking over the events of a difficult day. There had been a fight between the ship's pilot and the rest of the crew after the former announced that he had seen huge sandbanks rising from the water. He declared that it was the island of Diego Garcia; they insisted that they were approaching the Maldives. The argument was interminable. Finally, Captain Grout made a fateful and fatal decision. They would sail between the sandbanks towards the Indian coast.

He leapt from his bed and hurried to the bridge. The *Hammer* had now struck twice against a huge rock and was tipping over on its side, falling into the sand. As the helmsman shakily clutched an empty bottle and snored with his head tucked between two beams, the captain watched the rest of his sleepy, drunken crew awaken with terror. As they discovered the extent of the disaster, they wept and begged salvation from the saints. Leaving the others to seek divine assistance, the hardiest sailors cut down the masts to keep the ship from tipping over any further. Captain Grout struggled to take control of the situation, and fired a cannon shot to warn the *Crescent* of the danger ahead.

As dawn approached, the tearful crew watched the *Crescent* sail past, unable to save them. There was nothing to do. Captain Grout surveyed the enormity of the wreckage, immobile as if he had been turned to stone. Pyrard de Laval and a few other sailors decided to make rafts from the ship's planks. A few hours later, the crew was greeted by the inhabitants of the island. Their weapons were seized and they were taken prisoners. Their captors dispersed them on different atolls. Mathurin Picav and Pyrard de Laval were imprisoned together on an island called Pandouai.

Mathurin's dreams had shattered against the coral reefs. At first, he was so disheartened that he could only languish in a hut while Pyrard worked for their survival. Left to scrounge for food, they sustained themselves on snails and dead fish that the waves tossed ashore. They boiled seawater and strange herbs. Tatters of sails were the doors of their hut; its sides were open to the wind and rain. Mathurin and his friend fell gravely ill. The inhabitants of the island began to pity them, and gave

Pyrard coconuts, honey and millet. The young sailor took the opportunity to learn something of their language.

One day, fate turned in Pyrard's favour. He caught the eye of the nobleman Ali Pandio Atakuru. Ali found Pyrard an agreeable companion. He presented the Frenchman to an envoy from the royal court who had been sent to inspect the *Hammer*'s wreckage and report on the condition of its captive crew. The envoy was likewise charmed by the sailor's fine manners and wide knowledge of the world. He wanted to introduce Pyrard to his lord, but Pyrard insisted that he would not leave for court without his fellow in misfortune. Touched by this noble and magnanimous gesture, the envoy accepted Pyrard's request and took Mathurin with him to Malé.

Here the gallant and cultivated Pyrard won the heart of the island's sovereign, who sheltered him in his own palace. The sailor visited the royal couple every day, acquainting them with the customs of his homeland. While the king asked him about the French army and navy, the queen wanted to know about the dresses and character of the country's ladies. Charmed by Pyrard's elegance, the king lent him money to set himself up as a merchant.

Pyrard soon discovered that he had the makings of a perceptive trader. His business prospered. The foreign ships that passed by the island were his speciality. Those aboard fell under his spell and even left their goods in his care, asking him to negotiate with the locals on their behalf.

Now Pyrard was swimming in wealth. But he didn't forget his companion.

On a winter's night, two guards came looking for Mathurin Picav while he shivered in his dirty cabin. With fear in his belly, he followed the men through the dark street that led to the palace. The sound of the *bodu beru* echoed in the night, accompanying his slow steps. Cold drops of sweat formed pearls on his forehead; he shivered uncontrollably. A few days before, he had watched the execution of some of the sailors who had attempted to escape. Rumour had it that the king was considering having a few more killed for good measure. Mathurin panicked as he passed the Great Mosque. He knew that at the end of the next side street lay the prison where his companions had been killed.

He was shocked when his guards halted next to the prison, in front of a large house. They led him inside to a dark room lit by a single weak lamp, and left him beside the motionless body of Pyrard de Laval. The young sailor was laid out in bed, suffering from a terrible fever. Worried that his protégé required care that only a countryman could provide, the ruler had ordered one of his former crew members to be sent to him. So the role of Pyrard's nurse fell to Mathurin, who was only too happy to escape his own misery.

The peasant's devotion soon had an effect.

Carefully following the local medical wisdom, which called for potions of warm water and crushed pepper, Mathurin managed to lower Pyrard's fever. But hardly had this improved when Pyrard's legs began to swell grotesquely, and his vision faded almost to the point of blindness. Four months of convalescence followed. Pyrard was convinced that he had escaped death's clutches solely through the vigilant care of Mathurin. He persuaded the king to keep Mathurin on in his service. The two were now inseparable. Mathurin, whom Pyrard had taught to read and write, became the merchant's right-hand man.

Six years went by. Although they hoped to return home, Mathurin and Pyrard lived peacefully as they waited for a miracle. When it arrived, it wore a hideous disguise.

Mathurin Picav woke to shouts of alarm and echoes of frantic footsteps. He leapt from his bed and rushed out of the room into the hall. No sooner had he lit the lamp than he heard a rhythmic thudding in the street. Soldiers were running past. Pyrard had just stepped out of his own room, torn from sleep by the noise. The two men hurried to the palace, wondering what was about to unfold.

Earlier that evening, the watchmen on the coast had spotted a fleet of sixteen ships headed towards Malé. The king had reacted swiftly. He put seven galleys to sea, along with a number of smaller ships that were always kept at the ready for such cases. This wasn't the first time a ruler of the Maldives had faced a surprise attack.

By the time Mathurin and Pyrard arrived at the palace, they saw the ruler already heading down the steps accompanied by his wife and concubines, who sadly made their way to the royal galley. The king stepped towards Pyrard, and placed his hand on the sailor's shoulder. Pyrard was afraid the king would ask him to accompany them; here was his chance, at last, to escape. The king, with a tear in his eye, understood. A great wind arose and the royal galley set sail. While terror gripped the inhabitants of Malé, Mathurin and Pyrard began to dream of freedom.

As they realized their king had taken flight, hundreds of men, women and children scattered in terror, running in every direction but headed nowhere. The sound of the waves that carried the enemy ships was lost amid their screams. Pyrard and some of his companions surrendered to the invaders – who treated them roughly, suspecting them of being Portuguese. Once they had gotten over this false impression, the leader of the invading fleet called for Pyrard to be brought to his flagship. He treated the Frenchman with every courtesy.

The sailors embarked towards an unknown port. It was hard to enjoy their liberty under such conditions. After several weeks of sailing, the fleet put in at Chittagong in Bengal. They were received by the governor, who promised to help Pyrard and his companions find transit to Calicut and from there back to France. They were overjoyed. Six years of captivity were over. Deliverance appeared like the first rays of dawn. But some fates are written in shadow.

After a short stay in Calicut, Pyrard and his fellow travellers sailed to Cochin, where they hoped to find a ship bound for

France. But the deal they had struck with some Portuguese sailors turned to their disadvantage. As soon as they arrived in Cochin, they were bound hand and foot and thrown into the notorious *Le Tronco*: a high, square-set tower known for its filthy, sickly cells. The prison had no doors. Instead there was a board in the roof, held in place by four cords that were used to lower prisoners into the depths of *Le Tronco*. The unfortunates were fed through a window; the guards passed a long-handled bucket through its iron bars.

Mathurin fell into a deep, deep despair. Getting rich had been a horrible illusion, and now even returning home seemed impossible. He thought of the family he had left behind. In his solitude, however, he became aware of an old Dutchman mouldering in a neighbouring cell. The other prisoners thought him mad, but Mathurin discovered that this was only a ruse. To escape the guards' abuse, the old man had taken refuge in an imaginary world of pirates, demons and monsters. He appreciated Mathurin's kindness, and revealed to him a secret that would change his life.

The Dutchman had been one of the first merchants to collaborate with the Portuguese in their operations in the diamond mines of Masulipatnam. For many years, he had walked among the pits of Kollur, Cuddapah and Sambalpur. He had worked for the Sultan of Bijapur himself, and even worked the mines of Panna. From a mere adventurer, he had become a magnate, a 'farmer'. At that time, the right to exploit mines owned by a king or sultan was leased out to 'farmers', intermediaries between the ruler and the overseers. The position was a critical one; the farmer had the trust of the king and the respect of the merchants. The Dutchman's life would have been one of ease and power if he hadn't been so unlucky as to fall in love with one of the sultan's concubines. His attempt to escape on a Portuguese vessel was of no avail; he was thrown into *Le Tronco* and forgotten.

When Pyrard and Mathurin were set free – thanks to the intercession of the local Jesuits – Mathurin was determined to become a diamond trader himself. But fate hadn't had its final word. While they were still celebrating the news of their liberation, the governor of Cochin promised them that they would be put on the next ship to Goa. When they arrived at Goa, however, they were thrown into prison once again before being drafted into the Portuguese army.

Freedom finally came for them two years later. Four vessels were to set sail from Goa and they had been hired as servants on board. Mathurin sat in the tavern of Porto Bello, sunk in thought. The idea of returning home didn't agree with him. What would he tell his family? That his whole adventure had been nothing but misfortune and pain? That all he had seen of the world were the walls of different prisons? That his life was a failure?

When Pyrard found him, Mathurin was in torment. He had just made a tremendous decision. He would stay in India.

He wouldn't return to France until he was rich. Pyrard felt betrayed. Just as their misfortune was about to end, the friend with whom he had survived so many hardships was abandoning him. All night he tried to persuade his friend that he was making a mistake. But Mathurin's eyes shone like the diamonds of the Dutchman's stories. He spoke of his plans in a manic rapture. He would go to Golconda. Then at the zenith of its fortunes, Golconda held an inexhaustible wealth of gems.

But things took a bad turn when Mathurin met a man named Jean-Baptiste Tavernier...

8

Gilbert Thaata fell silent as he noticed a shadow stop in front of the house. It was Father Trémond, priest of the St. Francis Church. He stepped down wearily from his bicycle. The old Raleigh was now just a hunk of metal, still moving forward by a special act of divine grace.

It wasn't just the bicycle. Poverty seeped out of every pore of Father Trémond's body. The warped frame of his glasses was held together with tape. The arms were missing, replaced with pieces of string tied together behind his head. He never wore his cassock outside the church; he was afraid of getting it dirty – and how would he replace it? His robust frame, bushy beard and surly demeanour would have frightened anyone who didn't know him. But he had a pure soul, dedicated since childhood to God and the poorest of the poor. He was a man of unshakeable conviction.

The priest set his bicycle against the thinnai and briefly stretched his legs. He took a handkerchief out of his pocket and wiped the sweat from the back of his neck. He sat down in the chair that Lourdes offered him, and said with a huge grin, 'How are you, child? It's been a long time.'

'By the grace of God, Father, all's fine,' she said as she crossed herself. 'Do you want some water?'

'Have you lost your mind, girl!' Father Trémond's face reddened as he stared at the whisky bottle. 'Have you ever seen me drinking water at such an hour?'

'Lourdes, get the priest a glass of whisky,' my father added, as the frightened girl ran to the kitchen. Then he got up and moved his chair to make more room for Father Trémond.

'No, no. Don't bother, Paulin. Don't you trouble yourself, I'll sit where I am. So what are you talking about?' His glance fell on Gilbert Thaata. He stared at the old man for a long time, intrigued. He was used to all sorts of vagabonds taking refuge in our thinnai. But a wanderer like Gilbert Thaata was a rare sight in our neighbourhood. A thousand questions tingled on his lips. Out of respect for my father, he forced them back. He turned his attention instead to the glass of whisky my father held out to him. He took the glass and turned it slowly in his right hand. He sipped, waited ten seconds and then swallowed, clacking his tongue against the roof of his mouth. He smiled radiantly.

'Mmm. Nothing like a good Bagpiper. It's been a while. Here, tchin-tchin, Paulin,' he said with a wink. He held the glass under his nose and breathed in deeply several times. Finally, he raised his glass and turned again to the old man.

'To your health, Monsieur...'

Gilbert Thaata was taken aback by the priest's friendliness. He threw him a furtive look and mumbled, 'Um, you can just call me what everyone else does, Father.'

'Yes, but you do have a name, don't you?' The response was brutally inquisitorial.

Distraught, the old man tried to respond. No words came from his mouth. He looked beggingly at my father, who didn't have time to say anything.

'To your health, then, Gilbert Thaata.' The jovial voice of Father Trémond echoed strangely in the street. He drained the contents of his glass and stuck his fork in the plate that Lourdes had brought him. He closed his eyes and savoured the meat.

'Oh, my little Lourdes, may heaven bless you, child! God in his kindness has given you hands of gold. What a cook!' Father Trémond lifted his head heavenwards. 'Isn't it so, Paulin? What were you talking about?' The question was meant for the old man. Gilbert Thaata was uncomfortable. He didn't like this pushy, chummy priest. He felt like his place in the spotlight was being stolen. He laughed nervously instead of answering. He was afraid he would have to start his story all over. He looked to my father, silently asking him to end this embarrassing situation.

My father responded laconically, 'Oh, we were talking about this and that, Father. Nothing too special. Gilbert Thaata was just telling us his story. And what's your news, Father?'

'The same thing, Paulin, the same thing,' the priest replied as he patted the pockets of his shirt. He rose and began fumbling in his pants pockets.

'What are you looking for, Father?'

'I had a cigar in my pocket; now I can't find the thing anywhere,' he grumbled.

'Look, I've got one if you want it, Father.' Gilbert Thaata offered him a suruttu. He tried to make up for having imprudently wilted under the priest's stare a minute before.

'Thanks, thanks, Gilbert Thaata,' he said as he sat back down. 'But do you have one for yourself?'

'Oh, I've got enough, Father. Monsieur just bought a whole pack for me,' the old man said. He was relieved that the priest was speaking to him like everyone else did. That meant he wasn't suspicious any more. There would be no more inquisitorial looks.

Father Trémond lit his cigar and said to my father, 'Paulin, it's always the same problem. Money. What can I do? The diocese of Pondicherry only gives money to the big churches that already have it. Look at Sacré Coeur, Samba Covil. They have plenty. What they collect on a Sunday is already enough. And then they have the print shop, the schools, the nursery and everything else making money for them. And what do I have? What about me? A crumbling old church in a village of fishermen. Begging poor buggers for donations. An orphanage

I pay for out of my own pocket, from my own pension. I can't take money from these poor people and give it to the diocese – they'll give it to priests who eat biryani every Sunday. Look at this bicycle – it's as old as I am. And when I ask for money, the diocese complains. They say I don't make enough converts to expand the church. If my church is poor, there must be a reason... and then they invoke the good Lord! I know him, their good Lord. The bottles of red wine they sip all day. The roast chickens. The banknotes with Gandhi's toothy smile that slide under their cassock. I know who their God is, Paulin.' Father Trémond stopped, exhausted by his monologue.

Father Trémond cursed the whole world that he had been made the priest of this church that he loved so much. My father was his only friend.

He held out his empty glass towards my father. Whisky poured from the bottle with a reassuring glug.

'You must forgive me, Gilbert Thaata, I'm just tired. Don't pay any attention to what I'm saying. You can continue your story. It'll help me relax. It's not a problem if I don't know how it started.'

Gilbert Thaata was disconcerted. He had dropped the thread of his tale, and it would be hard to find it again after this stormy interruption. For a long time he seemed to be thinking; then he desperately shook his head. Where had he stopped?

'Jean Tavernier!' The name leapt from my brother's lips.

Everyone turned to stare at him.

'Jean Tavernier,' he repeated. 'You were saying that your ancestor's life changed when he met Jean Tavernier.'

'Well said, little one,' answered the old man. 'Yes, I stopped just as he was about to begin his next voyage.'

He straightened his shoulders, cleared his throat and continued his story. Now, with an additional listener – a difficult character at that – he had to adjust the tale. Father Trémond might turn out to be a critic as well as an inquisitor. He would have to double his efforts; no mistakes, no getting carried away. He had to be precise, clear, objective.

But Gilbert Thaata knew his art. His story, with sips of whisky and puffs of his cigar, held us spellbound. We were dazzled by his memory. How could he recall the smallest details of events that had happened centuries ago?

The street was empty. Lazy dogs yawned and searched for a place to sleep. The little group under the lamp post dispersed. Only Three-Balls Six-Faces, Little Gilbert and Khrushchev were left, plotting something. We finished eating and waited for the rest of the story. My father looked down at us, made sure we were still awake and told Lourdes to bring him another bottle of whisky.

'Jean-Baptiste Tavernier was now travelling to India for the second time...'

'Wait, Grandpa! So don't start without me now.' Lourdes's voice rang from the kitchen. She reappeared with a bottle tucked under her arm and three plates of grilled meat in her hands.

'So then, Jean-Baptiste Tavernier was travelling to India for the second time. But it was his first trip to Golconda. Before then, he'd been in Agra with Shah Jahan. He was mad for diamonds. So he went to the Sultan of Golconda, Abdullah Qutb Shah, who introduced him to my ancestor. As soon as they met, the two men took a liking to each other. Mathurin Picav hadn't seen another Frenchman for a long time. And Jean-Baptiste Tavernier was a good man to know. He showed my ancestors all kinds of techniques for cutting and polishing gems…'

Tavernier came and went. Mathurin had profited from his relationship with the adventurer to send a message – and a considerable sum of money – to his family in France, who had heard nothing from him for many years. By the time Tavernier returned to India on his fourth voyage, Mathurin – now a rich man – was burning with longing for his homeland. But it was then that Tavernier spoke of a mysterious gemstone hidden in a temple: the Stone of Sita.

Along the Krishna river lay the ruins of an ancient shrine dedicated to Rama, abandoned since the invasion of Qutb Shahi. There were many dreadful rumours about the place. Skeletons scattered around the temple grounds were testaments to its sinister character. Villagers avoided it.

Who knows what tapestry Mathurin's brain was weaving?

A few days later, he left town with Tavernier. The latter had taken care of everything. As the men boarded a ship for Europe, no one knew that the stone was missing. In the shadows of their cabin, it gleamed like moonlight. The dream Mathurin had nursed in *Le Tronco* was coming true. A single diamond cast the prison walls and all its thousands of stones into oblivion…

Gilbert's voice echoed in the night. Here and there snores rose from neighbours' houses. The dogs were now asleep. The whole neighbourhood was silent. There was only the rustle of the naga's leaves in the wind. Gilbert Thaata was exhausted from the effort of remembering so many details over the centuries – or from the effects of his whisky. He paused and scratched his beard. He had chosen his moment well. He knew that all through the night, our spirits would keep wandering through the story of his grandfather.

Father Trémond had fallen asleep in his chair. The sudden silence woke him. He returned his empty glass to Lourdes and stood up.

'Goodnight, Paulin. I'm heading home. It's been a long day.'

'Goodnight, Father! And, hey, take the bicycle to Ramu's shop tomorrow. I'll pay for the repairs. You can't go on like this. One of these days you'll be left holding just the handle.'

'Thanks, Paulin, but I'd rather you buy a new neon light for the church's entrance. For three days now it's been looking like an abandoned building. I'll come back tomorrow.' He vanished around the corner.

My father sighed and turned back to us. 'Okay boys. That's it for today. It's late. Get to bed.'

'But Papa, the story isn't over yet,' my brother answered, blinking hard to ward off the drowsiness that was creeping upon him.

I was already cast away on a coral reef of some dream kingdom. Pirates had captured the ship of my consciousness, and were taking it away to unknown shores.

9

'Sita's curse came quickly. As they sailed back to France, negotiations began and soon turned bitter. Tavernier wanted the diamond for himself. He could sell it to Louis XIV for a huge profit – the king had a passion for diamonds. It was an enormous stone, 112 carats, in the shape of a triangle – a rare beauty with a deep blue colour, almost purple. Millions of years old, born in the bowels of the Deccan plateau, inching upwards out of the earth one volcanic eruption at a time to come to light one day along the Krishna. But Jean-Baptiste Tavernier was an honourable man. He wouldn't even consider using dirty tricks to get the diamond.'

Gilbert Thaata continues his story. My father had caught a fever for it. Like the previous day, he had come home early today with meats from Maleappa. As he spread out the slices of ham-and-garlic sausages, the old man couldn't help but smack his lips in pleasure. He hurriedly dismissed Asamandi Baiyacaca Sonal, who was fighting Afars and Issars in Africa for the thousandth time. He knew that the coming day would be a happy one. He would stretch the story out as long as he could.

Everyone was in their usual places: my father in the little thinnai and we by his side; Lourdes sitting in the doorway, ready to run back and forth from the thinnai to the kitchen; Kaatannan had joined today and was sitting on the edge of the thinnai beside the old man.

'Wait, old-timer,' interrupted my father. 'Father Trémond said he'd come by. Shouldn't we wait for him? He seemed to like your story.'

'If you wish, sir,' the old man answered hesitatingly. He tried to contain his disappointment. He didn't feel comfortable with this priest around. When Father Trémond was there, he kept to his story, instead of interrupting himself to make remarks or give orders to Little Gilbert. Clutching his glass, he stared dreamingly into the distance. His blue eyes were looking for secret memories.

Three-Balls Six-Faces was starting his show. The pleasure of the little group of spectators was interrupted by Selvanadin's father, who appeared at the end of the street, swaggering drunk. He stopped in front of Pattakka's shop and began insulting her. This went on for a few minutes until she brandished her ladle at him and he decided to move along. As he turned away from her, he nearly tripped into her pot of boiling oil. One of Manickam Annan's sons, Boulkani, happened to be there and grabbed him by the arm. This enraged Selvanadin's father, who took off his kaili and got himself ready for a fight.

'So that's how you want it? You want to fight the biggest *vaatiyar* in Kurusukuppam? I may look old, but I can take on any of you. Come on! Show me what you can do,' Selvanadin's father said defiantly. Surprised and disappointed that the young man remained silent, he picked up his kaili and added, 'Homo! Bastard! Son of a bitch! You can't even fight an old man. You're just a sissy! Your father is a homo, you're a homo and your whole family is a bunch of homos.'

Tripping over his kaili, he seemed as if he was going to walk away. But after a few steps he turned to the group of onlookers and began muttering a string of curses. Then, with no warning, he rushed towards Boulkani. The young man watched him without raising an eyebrow. When the old man had almost reached him, he stepped aside. Selvanadin's father crashed face-first against a wall.

The crowd around Pattakka's shop exploded in laughter. The boys with Three-Balls Six-Faces under the lamp post rushed over to catch the show. When they saw Selvanadin's father lying on the ground, they began throwing sand at him, clapping and shouting, riling him up.

'Go on, vaatiyar! Show him that you can still fight! Show us you're still the toughest in the neighbourhood!'

The old cook wobbled to his feet and said, 'Oh, you pushed me against the wall, you damned homo! You don't know how to fight like a real man. I'll teach you, I will!'

The boys danced around mockingly, throwing sand and stones and pushing him towards Boulkani.

'So what are you waiting for? Come on, once I've finished with you, I'll go fuck that dirty whore, your mo–'

He didn't have time to finish. The young man planted a fist in his face. Blood spurted from his lip and a second later he fainted.

The boys exulted. 'Hey! Vaatiyar fell!' They kicked the old man as he lay motionless in the dirt. Boulkani took Selvanadin's father's arm and dragged him home. Then he set him against the little thinnai of his house as Selvanadin's sisters looked on, heartbroken. The old cook regained consciousness and said to Boulkani, 'Thanks, Thambi! I'm lucky you're here. Manickam Annan's son just hit me!'

Gilbert Thaata turned towards my father, disgusted.

'How can you live in this neighbourhood? Aren't you afraid for your children?'

'I know, old one. It's not an easy place to live in. But I'm from here. This is where I learned about life. People are ignorant, violent and quarrelsome here. But they have something that people in "nice neighbourhoods" don't. Honesty! At least here my boys know where they stand.'

As I was mulling over my father's answer, Father Trémond appeared. He stopped at the lamp post to chide the boys, who stood with their arms crossed. He moved towards the house muttering something. He sat down in his usual spot, wiping the sweat from his forehead and neck. He had only just greeted my father when he rose again and set off for Marie-Madeleine's shack. After a few minutes, the preacher's voice could be heard at a growing volume. When he left her hovel, his face was red with fury.

'What is it, Father? You seem upset,' my father asked.

'Oh, Paulin, those people are going to take my skin one of these days! My skin, my skin, that's all I have left… It's been a month since she gave birth to that poor creature, and she still hasn't baptized him. God knows the child will need it. I sent over the sacristan several times to convince her to let us baptize the baby, but she refuses.'

'Why?'

'Who knows!' he said, raising his arms towards heaven. 'Who knows what goes through the head of that woman. And what's more, she has the nerve to tell me that if baptism is just a matter of giving her son a name, well, the neighbourhood takes care of that. She told me that the child is called Emile Something-Head… I don't remember Paulin, Emile Something-Head.'

'Yes, but baptism isn't just a matter of a name. There's a whole ceremony, a symbolism and the witnesses that make the child part of the Christian community.'

'I told her all that, *mon vieux*! You know what she said to me? "If your ceremony is just pouring water on my son's head, go ahead and pour some water and get it over with." She handed me a glass of water, Paulin! I could have smashed that glass… I told her it had to be holy water. So she asked me what makes the water holy. It's been blessed, I told her. She asked me who blessed it. I stared at her. Rolling my eyes, I said, "What do you mean, who blesses it? A priest, for Christ's sake!" She looked at me and said, "So bless this glass of water, pour it on my son and then it's over. I'm not going to waste my money on all this churchy play-acting."'

My father burst into laughter. 'She's not all wrong, Father.'

'Don't you get mixed up in this, Paulin! The Devil is living in that woman. She deserves her name. May God protect her.' Father Trémond glared angrily at her shack. 'And what's the matter with her child?'

Seeing that no one answered his question, Lourdes responded.

'It was the full moon, Father.'

'What in God's name? You can't believe in this sort of story. When are you people going to put an end to these superstitions!' The priest barked as he slapped his thigh.

Lourdes fled inside the house. When she returned carrying a glass for him, Father Trémond seemed to have calmed down.

'Don't be afraid, child. I'm not angry with you. I'm just a little annoyed.' He patted her head to reassure her.

After serving him a plate of charcuterie, Lourdes returned to the doorway.

'Mmm...better and better. Today it's charcuterie. You're lucky, old-timer,' Father Trémond said to Gilbert Thaata while keeping his eyes on his plate. 'Good fortune has brought you to the house of an honest man who loves stories. As long as you have a tale to tell, he'll spoil you. Try to keep yours going for as long as possible so that everyone can benefit.'

He shot a mocking glance at my father and swallowed a bite of sausage. He raised his glass.

'Tchin-tchin, Paulin. You know I'm joking. *Santé*, old-timer! Where did your tale leave off?'

'Uh...I was talking about my ancestor. I was just about to finish his voyage...' Gilbert Thaata responded evasively, cutting a piece of sausage and greedily devouring it. He wiped the crumbs from his white beard, lit a cigar and continued his story.

'The days went by. The boat was nearing French shores, but the negotiations still continued. I think Mathurin Picav didn't even want to sell the diamond...'

But a few days before their arrival in France, the inevitable finally happened. One morning, Jean-Baptiste Tavernier started to get nervous that he hadn't seen Mathurin. He sent a servant to look for him. The servant returned a few minutes later, screaming. The old sailor lay dead in his cabin.

Pushing the onlookers aside, Tavernier entered the room. He thought of the diamond. No one else knew it existed. Everyone thought Mathurin had died a natural death. His belongings were gathered and handed over to the captain, who would be responsible for sending them to his family.

Tavernier anxiously wondered how to get his hands on the diamond. But when the ship arrived at port, his hopes of recovering the stone disappeared as he watched my ancestor's possessions being loaded onto the back of a carriage. Tormented by his loss, Tavernier paced along the docks, moving through the bustling crowd while trying to think of some solution.

He was surprised when a fellow sailor – a confidant of Mathurin's – called out to him, gesturing him to come to a nearby tavern. Following nervously, Tavernier entered a dark room. Curiosity overcame his suspicion. They moved into a shadowy corner where darkness hid the sailor's guilty, sickening grin. Out of the other patrons' sight, the man opened a dirty handkerchief to reveal the diamond.

Tavernier took a step backward, struck with fear. The diamond shone like a star in the sailor's thick and soiled fingers and bathed his face in a violet gleam. The sailor, already drunk, admitted his crime. He had poisoned Mathurin. Tavernier's first thought was to shout for the police. But if they came, Tavernier would never recover the diamond…

'Do you mind, sir?' Gilbert Thaata asked as he clutched his cane. He tried to get up, but his legs had fallen asleep. He trembled. Lourdes reached out and helped him to stand.

'Thank you, Lourdes,' he said, tapping her on the shoulder. 'Where's that damn boy? Gilbert!' the old man shouted in the direction of the lamp post. 'Hey, Fat Gilbert, come here!' He turned back to Lourdes with a wink.

'I'm afraid he fall,' Lourdes said to my father in a tone of censure. 'That's what it is, sir. That boy don't do even nothing. Eat, sleep, play movies with Three-Balls Six-Faces...so.' She caught sight of Little Gilbert. 'Come now, take Grandpa to the garden, good-for-nothing!'

In Kurusukuppam, 'going to the garden' was a euphemism. Only Monsieur Michel's and our house had toilets. Everyone else went to the 'garden', the coconut grove. You could see silhouettes hiding behind the trees all day long.

The old man and the boy went off. Lourdes entered the house and came back with a box of matches. She lit the thinnai's oil lamp. She scared away a gecko that was swallowing mosquitoes, stepped down and turned to my father.

'Poor Grandpa! He suffers a lot for money, Monsieur. And that fat boy steals him. He buys half bottle of sarayam and fills it with water. He takes money for the movies. One day I cut his dick off. Grandpa has too much pain, he's a nice monsieur. You, you Monsieur, talk to Little Gilbert. He doesn't listen me –'

'Okay, Lourdes, calm down. I'll talk to him,' my father interrupted Lourdes's speech. When she was worked up like that, she could talk forever. And she kept talking as she went back into the house.

'Grandpa is sad...so his health...' The words faded in the darkened sitting room.

'It's time we get that girl married. We can't keep her here forever,' Papa said to Kaatannan and sighed meaningfully. 'She needs to make a life for herself.'

'Sure, you're right. But where would you find a husband for her? It'd have to be someone from her own community...and besides, with her character...' Kaatannan whispered.

'Oh, Kaatu, she's not a bad girl. She's just a little independent-minded. Okay, she's difficult, but she's good.'

'No one heard of the diamond again until...' Gilbert Thaata had returned to the thinnai and his tale. Little Gilbert put the old man's cane next to the bundle on which he was sitting. He looked annoyed. The fun with Three-Balls Six-Faces was over. The spectators had gone home. There were only insects under the lamp post. There was silence in the street, except for the sound of a dog scratching itself.

'Even today, I have the feeling that my ancestor, without knowing it, played an important part in our country's history. I can't imagine what its fate might have been if he hadn't stolen that diamond from a lost temple of Golconda...'

Of all the kings of Europe, no one could spend money like Louis XIV. And he adored diamonds. One night, in 1668, he received Tavernier in the palace. He purchased forty large diamonds and 1,200 small ones. But as the evening drew to a close, he was still unsatisfied. He already regretted having listened to the ministers who had praised this merchant. But then Tavernier extended his hand, and Louis XIV shouted in astonishment. Filling Tavernier's palm was the shimmering beauty of the Stone of Sita. The king was conquered by its mysterious enchantment. He didn't know that it could be a danger to its owners.

Louis XIV passed it on to Louis XV, who passed it on to Louis XVI... And then the French Revolution came. The royal family tried to escape the kingdom, and their treasures were confiscated by the new government. The National Assembly decided that the people should know about this wealth that they now owned. So the precious gems and other finery were brought out for display every Monday. But one night in September 1792, a band of thieves made their way into the treasury...

Gilbert Thaata stopped a moment and extended his glass towards Lourdes, who quickly filled it. We were getting used to his pauses. They meant that some major event or exciting turn was about to take place. He took a sip and cleared his throat. My father lit another cigarette.

'The Stone of Sita was never seen again. But its disappearance cost Louis XVI his life. On 22 September 1792, the government abolished the monarchy and declared that the French Republic was born…

'My family, however, didn't know what had happened to the diamond. After my ancestor's death, his wealth allowed them to leave farming for more profitable affairs. Some went to Brittany, to the port of Lorient where they began trading in imports from India. They became immensely rich...while business was good. Then there were jealousies, misunderstandings, quarrels... The family was divided.

'My grandfather left France for the Antilles, where the sugar business was then at its height. Somehow, since the theft of the diamond, my family has always been on the wrong side of history... They got involved in the slave trade. Maybe it's Sita's curse...'

Rain began falling. Lourdes barely had time to put away the chairs and plates. The smell of the soft, warm soil soaking up the rain spread throughout the neighbourhood. Droplets as big as hail pelted the few passers-by, some of whom ran for cover under the trembling roof of Karika Bhai's shop, others under Ramu's. Sad, soaked dogs searched for a dry corner.

10

Kurusukuppam was miserable in the rain. There were no canals. Dead animals and debris floated in the flooded streets. Children played with swollen carcasses of rats bobbing along the current. Adults sat on thinnais, trying to cover themselves with thin blankets. They couldn't stay indoors – water had already filled their homes, coming up from the street and down through leaky roofs.

Sitting in the thinnai, surrounded by refugees from the flood, Gilbert Thaata stared at a black, menacing sky dotted with rain clouds. Dripping crows tried to keep their balance on coconut trees that bent under the gale. While children set newspaper boats afloat on the water, adults looked sadly at the clouds and smoked beedis. Too poor to own umbrellas, many protected themselves with banana leaves held above their heads as they moved from one place to another. The sharp and bitter smell of *karuvadu* wafted from huts – this was the only dish that people could make on rainy days. The Great Bazaar was too far away.

Kurusukuppam was drowning in despair.

Everything had closed, even the main road that led to the inundated cemetery. But this didn't keep the men from the kallukadai. They crossed the street with huge leaps, as if it were a sporting field. Pattakka watched them sadly. A leaden silence struck the neighbourhood, broken by the shouts and cries of children whose exasperated parents – at the height of frustration and boredom – had begun to beat them.

At the end of the third day the rain stopped. A radiant sun lit the sky. Our thinnai was abandoned as its exiles returned to their lives. Gilbert Thaata was relieved. He insisted that the thinnai be thoroughly cleaned. Through the three days of rain, he had suffered greatly, having had nothing to smoke or drink. He waited impatiently for nightfall, watching the street for the first sign of my father's return.

The neighbourhood returned to its routine. Bored men were sitting on the bench in front of Ramu's shop listening to a song playing on an old Murphy radio. Women were squabbling and slapping each other around the fountain. Older children were clearing the football field, which the rains had covered in tree branches, palm fronds and other debris; younger ones were splashing in the few remaining puddles. The smell of fritters wafted in the breeze.

Pattakka's customers were watching Three-Balls Six-Faces. He was just about to rip Little Gilbert's face apart. The rain hadn't kept him from seeing *Adimai Penn*. Every year, one or another of the many cinemas showed this old MGR film. And every year, Three-Balls Six-Faces would re-enact it beneath the lamp post. Neither he nor anyone else in the neighbourhood ever got tired of seeing it. Whether in the cinema or in the street, everyone admired the climactic scene when the hero confronted a lion bare-handed – the scene Three-Balls Six-Faces was acting out now. Seated on Little Gilbert's back, Three-Balls Six-Faces' right hand gripped the boy's upper jaw and pulled his head back, while the left plunged into his mouth and pulled the lower jaw down. Little Gilbert writhed in pain. His groans resembled the roar of a lion, which encouraged the efforts of Three-Balls Six-Faces and the pleasure of the spectators.

The kallukadai's usual queue of visitors formed a jostling zigzag. The rain hadn't cleansed the neighbourhood. Everything was back to normal.

Kaatannan had just arrived at the house with a large bag from which the smell of biryani escaped. He stepped into the kitchen and set the bag down in front of Lourdes, who was busy cooking.

'Hey, who that now, what that now, how that go?'

'Look, Monsieur said to bring you this. There's no need to cook tonight.'

Lourdes turned from struggling with the damp wood that refused to catch fire and responded furiously.

'So what now, so now you come! Monsieur said me nothing! I started making food for tonight, the boys very hungry. So why Monsieur say to buy beef this morning? He never listen me. What that now?'

'It's biryani. The best, from Salem Biryani. Not like the stuff you make.' Kaatannan wrinkled his face in disgust.

'Watch out, Kaatannan, don't make that monkey face with me. I cut your tail off one day. Go now, put the bag here,' she said, gesturing to the table. 'And Monsieur eats here or at the hotel?'

'No, he's coming home. And he won't be long, either. He's at the Cercle with his friends. Give me another bag, I need to buy something for him to drink.'

'Cercle, Cercle. Always Cercle. What Monsieur thinks? This is hotel?'

Kaatannan stepped out. Before mounting his bike, he spoke to the old man.

'It's going to be a nice time for you, old-timer. Biryani on the menu, with red wine and whisky. Do you need suruttus too?'

He whistled a tune that faded in the twilight.

Gilbert Thaata seemed a younger man after a few glasses of whisky. He had devoured his plate of biryani in an instant, and now was savouring a cigar with a glass of wine. Three nights of sobriety and boredom had vanished. He was in a talkative mood. He began his story without needing to be asked.

'I had been born on a plantation in Capeterre, Guadeloupe. Since the decline of the family's trading business, one of my forefathers had gone into exile in the Antilles, where he hoped to remake his fortune in sugar production. It was 1760...'

Gilbert Thaata's ancestor had been described by him as a 'strong-willed' man – bull-headed and ambitious. He dreamed of getting rich, of owning a vast plantation. Unable to fulfil this fantasy, he passed on to his children the only inheritance he could give them: a feverish appetite for wealth.

The abolition of slavery in 1848 was a blow to the family. Most of their former slaves left the plantation as fast as they could. The whole family had to work in the fields. Their matriarch died, eaten away by worry. She left ten children behind her. Gilbert Thaata's father, gentle and defenceless, was the youngest. Abused by his father, mocked by his siblings, he escaped into a world of books. He was still too young and weak to work. Gradually, Gilbert's father, guiltily remembering his wife's death, left the boy alone. Far from paternal authority and the suffering workers, the boy spent his time in the library – a peaceful, solitary life.

As time went on, the family disintegrated. Girls were married into other families; boys left to start their own. Worn out by the old man's tyranny and greed, all the siblings had gone – except for two brothers. One was Gilbert's father.

The lives of the old man and his two sons were shaken one summer day by the arrival of an anonymous letter. It contained a secret unknown to any of them – one that recalled memories of Mathurin Picav.

When Gilbert Thaata's grandfather finished reading the letter, he grabbed the wrist of the first person he saw and gripped it tightly, covering his face with kisses and swaying beside him. 'We're rich, we're rich, we're finally rich!' The old man shouted again and again until he realized he was holding his unloved child. Blushing, he sidled away to find his other son.

Later that day the two brothers found their father in his room, packing. He was facing away from them, and didn't turn when they entered. This part of the house hadn't been aired out since their mother's funeral. A thick and acrid odour filled the room. Cobwebs dangled from the ceiling.

Overcoming their disgust, the brothers sat on the edge of their father's bed and realized with astonishment that he was preparing for a long voyage to France. He didn't tell them how long his absence would last.

All they knew for certain was that, upon his return, they would be rich.

11

On an August night in 1854, a man and a woman wandered the streets of Pondicherry. As they walked, the young couple looked around them in hesitation and fear. The man had a walking stick in his right hand, the woman held a fold of her sari over her head. Her other arm was carrying a heavy sack. She was sore beneath its weight and it began to droop against her side. Their uncertain steps slowed as they approached a temple. The woman gestured to the man.

'Pandyan, let's stop for a moment. I can't go on. I'm so tired. And...do you know where we're going?' She put the sack down without waiting for an answer.

'No more than you do, Tilaga. It's my first time here, too. Sit down on the bundle here. Rest a little. I'll go look around this temple and see if there's a place to sleep tonight.'

The woman, who had been just about to sit down, stood back up in protest.

'Oh no! I'm not staying on this sidewalk all by myself.'

The man took her tenderly in his arms.

'Tilaga dear, this is hard for me, too. You have to be strong. You have to trust me. Be reasonable. Just wait for me here, and I'll be right back. It won't be long.'

He left his wife waiting and headed towards the temple. But he had hardly gone more than a few metres when a man greeted him. This man had been watching the couple from across the street. He and Pandyan spoke for a moment that seemed very long to Tilaga. At last Pandyan returned, exultant.

'Tilaga! I think fortune is smiling on us now. Not only can this gentleman give us a place to sleep, but jobs, too, for both of us.'

Hidden beneath her makeshift veil, Tilaga looked sceptically at the man, who was chewing betel. Pandyan, euphoric, didn't notice her expression.

'Our prayers have been answered. We met him by the temple – it's a sign. This gentleman is offering us jobs overseas, a few days by ship from here. Everything is on the level: contract, salary, voyage. They take care of everything. We'll work for vellakarans on an island. This is our chance, Tilaga! Good fortune. God guides our way.'

'What will we do there? What kind of work is it? And why do we have to leave this country?'

Pandyan took her by the arm to the man, who had been standing off to the side. He said laughingly, 'Mister, tell her, tell her yourself. My wife won't believe me.'

The man spat betel juice against the wall. He wiped his mouth with the *tundu* that he carried on his left shoulder. His reddish smile struck Tilaga as an indefinite expression of evil.

'Dear lady, you have nothing to fear. It's easy work. You take sugar from the sugarcane plantations and you dry it. It's not a very long contract, just two or three years. You'll be housed, fed and paid. You can make a lot of money – you can get rich. It's not an opportunity to pass by, dear lady. If I were you, I wouldn't wait one second.'

The woman stared at him for a long time. The man felt uncomfortable and avoided her gaze. Pandyan spoke.

'What's bothering you, Tilaga? Why are you hesitating? Look, we only just got into town and already something good has happened to us. What are you afraid of? Nothing's going to happen. Trust me, darling. Anyway, we can't stay here long... Imagine if your father's family catches up with us. And they will, sooner or later. Let's leave now, while we can.'

Tilaga didn't know how to answer. Pandyan was right. If her father's kinsmen ever caught them, she perhaps would live. The whole business might be covered up. Her family could weave some story that she had gone to visit a distant relative, and everything would be settled. She'd be married off to the first acceptable suitor. But Pandyan's family would be beaten and ostracized by the village, and her lover's corpse would float in the river.

Pandyan couldn't wait any longer. He picked up the sack and began walking towards the man. Tilaga stood motionless for a few seconds, then followed.

But she had been right.

At first, Pandyan and Tilaga were taken to the office of an emigration agent, who made them sign contracts. Tilaga asked several times why they stipulated five years instead of the two or three that the man had said. The man responded testily. 'Three years, four years, five...sister, what's the difference? You don't count the years when you're getting rich. You'll see, you'll thank me when you make it there. Go on, sister, sign it. There are others waiting for me. Look now, Lakshmi is here, opening her arms wide to embrace you.' The emigration agent handed them the first two months of salary in advance. The sight of the money set Pandyan's face aglow.

'You see, Tilaga, there's nothing to worry about. We haven't even started working and they're already giving us money. There's no need to be afraid.' He took her in his arms.

The young woman was too preoccupied to rejoice.

The couple had to wait for over a month in the city godowns: dark enormous warehouses with wooden doors always shut. There were many of them along Boulevard Sud. Their living conditions were deplorable. From the moment that they had signed the contracts, she had felt as if they were prisoners. They were closely watched, and didn't have the right to leave the godown. The facility, with its locked gate and high walls, was in no way welcoming. And she was uneasy among people from so many different castes, under the lustful eyes of so many men. Some of the women who were in the godown were prostitutes, others widows or single mothers abandoned by their families – desperate souls fleeing poverty. Drugged and stolen children huddled in a corner.

At the end of September, the couple boarded the *Aurélie* along with 300 other passengers – mostly single men, but also a few women and children. As the ship left Pondicherry behind, Pandyan and Tilaga were plunged into uncertainty, straining for a last glimpse of a town they barely knew. The woman had been afraid when she first saw the ocean, panicked by its immensity and deafening roar. Pandyan had tried to comfort her. But as the boat left the shore, she became inconsolable. Pressed against Pandyan, she wept, sure that she would never see her homeland again.

The voyage lasted three months. When the ship docked at Pointe-à-Pitre on 26 December, Tilaga was relieved to have survived. But her tour of hell had just begun. It was only when they arrived that most of the passengers realized that they had come to replace the slaves. Once the administrative formalities were finished, they were distributed among their new masters. They were given booklets and certificates. Pandyan received two shirts, two pairs of pants and a straw hat; Tilaga two shirts, two skirts and two handkerchiefs for her head. Then they were led to the former slave cabins.

The long days began at sunrise. They were paid in copper coins marked with the initials of the *béké*, the plantation owner. These could only be used in the shop that he owned. Pandyan and Tilaga lived in wretched poverty like the other Indians. India seemed more and more remote.

After five years, they knew that they could never go back, and decided to accept this new country as their home. They signed several contracts with one master after another, nursing the hope of one day owning their own little plot of land. By 1870, they had saved enough to open a shop.

Tilaga was a natural businesswoman. All those around her admired her, and she had even won permission from the plantation owners to organize Hindu rituals around a makeshift temple. Thus, when she and Pandyan celebrated the puberty of their daughter, Neelavathi, a community festival was held.

In the moment of collective celebration, no one noticed the furtive figure hidden behind the temple admiring Neelavathi's beauty.

12

For several minutes, Gilbert Thaata had been thinking in silence. His expression was sombre. He put his hands on his dangling legs and sighed.

'Everything changed for my father when the old man left. After a few days, his brother realized that he couldn't run the plantation by himself. So he pushed my father out of the library where he had been hiding since childhood...

'A new world opened. He had only ever known the damp odour of old books; now he could smell the perfume of life. Leaves instead of pages; birdsong instead of words; hills and valleys instead of tables and chairs. He had never looked beyond the family estate. From the library window, his gaze stopped at the last of the servants' cabins. He had never felt any desire to go further.

'At first, everyone was surprised to see the pale and thin young man wandering around the plantation. Only the house servants knew who he was: the coolies had been unaware that my father even existed. He was awkward among the workers. He couldn't raise his voice to give orders. He didn't know how to ride a horse. All day long, under a wide straw hat that hid his face, he would walk back and forth over the plantation. His body, long and thin as a flute, disappeared amidst the sugarcane.

'By day's end he was always exhausted, as if he had been breathing in the workers' suffering. Guilt gnawed at him. He had known nothing of the miserable world in which he lived.

'After my grandfather left for France, my uncle felt sorry for my father and tried to include him in the running of the plantation. But he soon realized my father had neither the business sense nor authority with the workers to help out. If not his useless brother, then someone else would have to oversee the work. And the house was in disrepair. The old maid had fallen ill. Under the circumstances, my uncle made Pandyan his overseer and Tilaga the new maid.

'She refused. It was out of the question for her to return to work as a servant. Pandyan, as usual, tried to argue. This was an opportunity. Not only would he be the overseer, but they could live in the big house. Life would be easier for them and Neelavathi. Tilaga sighed and relented, worn out by her husband's determination.

'My father's heart trembled with surprise and delight when he realized that the girl he had admired from his hiding place behind the temple was now coming to live with him.

'How did my future parents meet? I have no answer...one day the news of Neelavathi's pregnancy struck the house like a bolt of lightning. The servants' quarter screamed and wept. My uncle spent the night with his head in his hands. Only my father kept calm. He was ready to accept his responsibilities.

'His brother reminded him that this was not the first time a bastard had been born on a plantation, and suggested that he refuse to recognize the child as his own. My father remained firm. His brother was bemused to see someone who had always seemed to stand at the threshold of invisibility showing such determination.

'Finally, my uncle accepted that the child, its mother and her parents would stay in the house until his father's return from France. They would deal with the consequences then.

'Four happy years passed. A child's shouts and laughter had replaced the old man's angry curses. My uncle's fears vanished and he came to love me. When he returned from the fields for lunch, he would take me in his arms, spin me around over his head and throw me in the air as my mother watched nervously. I played with his beard while he told me stories. When evening fell, I slept with my head on his shoulder. I still remember the sweet smell of his pipe filling the veranda. It was a peaceful time.

'I was confused when my *Mabo* – my nursemaid – came to me one night and took me from my father's house. I didn't know where we were going. After some time, she stopped in front of a cabin and pushed me inside. I wouldn't go further than the doorway, and looked around with suspicion. I couldn't see much. The sugarcane leaves were shuddering in the wind.

A few oil lamps revealed dark shadows sitting in front of the other cabins.

'I was afraid. I wanted to go back home. But then I saw my mother. What was she doing here? She lifted me in her arms and carried me into the house, where I saw my grandparents. I didn't understand why we were in this shack. Sitting in the back of the cabin, my mother put me in her lap and tried to help me fall asleep. But all through the night, I heard strange noises, snores and coughs. My mother said in a sweet, comforting voice that this wouldn't last long.

'I returned to the big house the same way I left. One night, very late, Mabo came for me. I was happy to see her again. I ran to her and hugged her tight. She stood by the door and talked with my grandparents. The adults had a long discussion. I could see the shadows of curious neighbours gathering around the cabin. My father, with threatening gestures, told them to go away. After what seemed like an eternity, I left. My mother and my grandparents stayed at the cabin door. They seemed relieved as they watched me go.

'But when we got to the big house my Mabo brought me to the servants' quarters. For the next several days, I saw neither my father nor my uncle. My Mabo's old husband took me out into the garden, keeping me hidden behind a tree or a shed. I was the centre of a mystery.

'One morning, my Mabo dressed me in my nicest clothes. She put my things in a suitcase and took me to a carriage that was waiting in front of the house. She hugged me again and again and gave me kisses covered in tears. Her hands were shaking as she set me down in the carriage. I didn't know what was happening. I began to panic.

'Her husband had been standing off to the side, tearing at a piece of straw from his hat. He walked over to the carriage and told his wife to go. As he sat down beside me and the carriage began to move, it was as though a mirror inside me had shattered. Its shimmering fragments reflected images of my mother, my father, my happy former life.

'I turned back to look at the big house. I saw a man in the window smoking a pipe, watching me go. I learned later that this was my grandfather – my father's father.

'The journey was silent. Nothing was said, no explanation given. From time to time, my Mabo's husband tried to comfort me, stroking my head with a heavy hand. But my tears had already dried. My heart had hardened. Having formed the idea that I would never see my family again, my mind was now busy taking in the passing countryside, the final images of my homeland.

'We came to the ocean. I was fascinated by the beautiful waves that unfurled before me – so many arms beckoning me to an unknown life. The carriage stopped at the port. The old man took out my suitcase as I stepped down. He looked around nervously as if expecting someone. The port swarmed with activity. I had never seen so many people. I held his hand tight.

'In an attempt to soothe me, the old man pointed towards the boat that would carry me far away. He told me I was lucky to have the chance to travel, to sail on the ocean and discover a new world.

'After some time, a middle-aged man appeared. He looked me over and spoke to the old man in a whisper. My Mabo's husband gave him my suitcase and kissed me on the cheek. He started to cry. The man watched the two of us with a sad expression, which made me feel a little better. At least he wouldn't be cruel.

'Through my tears, I watched the old man turn away and vanish in the crowd. The man took me by the hand and led me onto the boat. Once on board, I could see the old man waving to me with this straw hat. The man let me watch this last scene of my old life as he spoke with another passenger.

'The plank between the boat and the dock began to rise, but a voice called out: "Wait, wait! There's one more passenger!" The plank stopped moving. The man looked at it, then took me to our shared cabin.

'That night, alone, I tried not to fall asleep. The man had gone on deck for a stroll. Through the half-open door, I could see the moon and stars. I closed my eyes. Another man entered the cabin. I felt his presence. He drew near my bed and began to caress my head. I moved back. I knew his touch, his smell. I was afraid to open my eyes, afraid that this familiar feeling would end. I heard him murmuring my name in a voice no ocean's roar could cover. I opened my eyes.

'Moonlight fell on my father's face.

'As time went by, the memory of my childhood faded, leaving only a few images. Sometimes my Mabo flickered in and out of existence, or the smell of tobacco in a pipe carried me back to the veranda of the big house. But the face of my mother was carved in my heart. At first, my father said that she would soon join us in France. We would all live together. As I grew up, I understood that it had been a lie. Neither of us knew what happened to her. I didn't lack for anything. We had a comfortable life. Upon our arrival in France, we were taken in by one of my grandfather's cousins. She and her family lived in a huge house in Brittany, on the Gulf of Morbihan. Extremely rich members of the local bourgeoisie, they were horrified by the sight of a distant, penniless cousin and his half-blood illegitimate son.

'But it seems that such people need the poor in order to feel rich. Helping my father and me allowed them to show their friends the extent of their Christian charity. We were given a dark room near the servants' quarters. They forgot about us most of the time, but once in a while they invited us out of our lair to display their generosity. After some time, my father found work at a library...'

After flickering on and off all night, the lamp went off. Dogs barked. Woken by the noise, Asamandi Baiyacaca Sonal began swearing: 'Damn dogs! As if I didn't have enough trouble sleeping...' He readjusted his kaili and headed to the garden. On the way back, he found a rock and threw it at the dogs, managing to hit one. It barked and whined as it fled. Satisfied, he turned back to his shack. But on the way he saw that we were still in the thinnai, talking away. He approached, scratching his head.

'Why, Paulin, are you still awake?' His voice echoed in the night. He had noticed that the bottle wasn't empty. He took the little cloth that hung from his shoulder and was about to sit down beside Gilbert Thaata.

'If we're awake, it's because we're not asleep,' my father said between his teeth. 'We were just finishing. It's very late, after all.' He answered quickly and moved as if he were getting up. Turning to us he said, 'Lourdes, clean this up! And you, boys, it's time to sleep, go inside.' Everyone stretched and yawned.

Asamandi Baiyacaca Sonal was disappointed. 'Oh! I thought I could hear some of your story,' he said, tapping Gilbert Thaata on the shoulder. 'Since you've been giving him wine and whisky, the old man doesn't need me any more. Isn't it, Gilbert Thaata? French food, Creole cooking, all that stuff makes you forget all your old friends.'

Gilbert Thaata opened his mouth to respond to his mockery, but he saw my father gesturing him to silence. An uncomfortable hush fell over the thinnai and all of us looked at Asamandi Baiyacaca Sonal. He wasn't embarrassed in the least. He took out a box of matches from a fold of his kaili and lit a beedi he had been keeping behind his left ear. Lourdes hurried over to the lamp and blew it out. 'Ayio! No more oil now,' she observed sadly. Asamandi Baiyacaca Sonal's match was still burning between his fingers, casting its light on an unhappy face. He shook it until it went out and then walked home muttering. Everyone exhaled in relief.

'It's a good thing you made me hold myself back, sir. If not, I would have said what I think of him. Who does he take himself for? He never offered me anything. I'd never drink his nasty sarayam. It's true that he's the one who paid for it, but he didn't even share it with me. He always finished the bottle before I could get a glass down. And then he has the nerve to tell me I'm forgetting my friends. First of all, he's not my friend, and second, I'm not ungrateful, sir.' Gilbert Thaata's face burned red with fury beneath the lamp Lourdes had just relit.

'It's not important, old-timer. Forget it! There's no sense in getting angry over such things. You know that madman as well I do now. He's not a bad person, just an irritating one. Please go on with your story.'

'My childhood passed in Brittany,' Gilbert Thaata started again. 'The desire to find my mother grew stronger and stronger…

'One day I told my father that I had made a decision. I would go and find her. He knew that he couldn't stop me. And I knew that he knew more than he had told me. I had seen him reading letters alone before. I had looked in every drawer, scrutinized every piece of furniture; I had opened every page of every book in the library. But I had never found them.

'A few days before I was to begin my journey, my father came home from work with a chest under his arm. He set it beside the fireplace and asked me to sit with him. The glow of the flames illuminated his face. He unlocked the chest with a tiny key and slowly opened the lid. I was in anguish as I waited to hear the secret. He took out a letter from the chest and pushed it towards me.

'"Son," he began. His voice was weak. He coughed. "I knew that this day would come. Ever since I found you on the boat, I knew that sooner or later you would leave. It's your right. I'm sad, but happy; you are now the master of your fate. Your childhood has not been as happy as it could have been. But I tried my best. I hope I didn't fail you. I never answered your questions about your mother or your grandparents. I told you that we would all be together one day and live like other families do. Well, that was a lie! I'm sorry. I'll spend my life regretting it. But I didn't see any other way. I didn't want you to know the terrible truth at such a young age. Now you're an adult.

'"I knew that they were going to send you away. My brother had told me a week before that my father was sending you to France. I didn't understand why he was punishing you for something I had done. But I didn't have the courage to face him. My brother told me to go along with it; he'd find some way to help me. Two days before you were taken, he brought me a little box with a letter, a ticket for the boat and some money. He promised me that Neelavathi would join us soon. I could have told her, but I didn't. I was afraid she or her parents would let the secret out. So I followed my brother's plan.

'"When the carriage took you away, I was in the fields. My brother had told my father that it would be a good idea if I were far from the house, so that there wouldn't be any kind of scene. He had arranged for another cart to pick me up. He hugged me and told me to read the instructions in the letter. I couldn't look at it while I was being driven to the port. I kept thinking about Neelavathi. I couldn't even open the letter until I found you on the ship. The instructions were to go to Brittany, where one of my father's cousins could help us. My brother and Neelavathi would join us later.

'"When we got to Brittany another letter came. Your grandfather Pandyan had confronted my father. My father had him whipped. And so that night Pandyan set fire to the big house. It spread to the fields. My father, my brother, my Mabo and her husband all died. The coolies ran. The police never found out who was responsible.

'"Pandyan and his family searched for work, going from one plantation to another. Pandyan became a drunk, wandering the streets in search of rum. Tilaga and Neelavathi left Guadeloupe to return to India; they left Pandyan behind. For some time after, I would get letters from your mother asking about you, saying she wanted to join us. But they stopped after a few years. This is the last one she sent. I don't know what happened."

'My father stood up. I watched the fire die. I had been expecting some revelation. What good was a letter from ten years ago with no information? How would I find my mother? Had she forgotten me? Didn't she care? The fire had gone out by the time my father returned, carrying something in his right hand.

'"Son, my brother gave me this when I left Guadeloupe. It belongs to the family, and now that you're going, it belongs to you. You'll do what you think best with it, once you've heard the story."

'He placed a small bag in my palm and asked me to open it. My hands shook.

'At the bottom of the bag was a diamond. "That's the Stone of Sita, my son." Then he turned to relight the fire.

'I took the diamond out of the bag. It was a beautiful grey-blue stone that fired reddish flashes as I turned it. I was stupefied.

'As the dry wood crackled in the fire, my father began his story in a soft monotone.

'"Many generations have wondered what became of the Stone of Sita... The night it was stolen, a fight broke out among the thieves. Someone took the opportunity to make off with the stone. And then one day, my father got a letter, the one that sent him back to France. It was from an old, old woman who was looking for information about the descendants of Mathurin Picav. As he read the letter, my father learned that his ancestor Mathurin had found an enormous diamond during his travels in India. The woman had heard the story from her grandmother. In her old age she turned to religion and renounced the world.

Fearing God's wrath, she decided to return the diamond to its rightful owners.

'"Why did my father come back to Guadeloupe with the diamond? Why didn't he sell it? I have no idea. He told my brother the story, and my brother gave it to us to help us start a new life in France. But I could never sell it either. I used to be tempted to go to India, find your mother and return the stone to Sita's temple. But I wasn't brave enough for that. Now you are going far away from me; the stone belongs to you."

'Day was breaking as my father finished his story. I was afraid of the new life I was now beginning, a life begun under such a sign. My father opened the curtains. I covered my face with my arm like a vampire while the Stone of Sita shimmered.'

13

'Sir, do you know what a meaningless life is?' The question surprised my father.

He was sitting in the thinnai with a glass in his hand.

Gilbert Thaata shuddered. Whisky was already taking him back to the far-off lands he had left behind. He had lost the thread of his story.

'Love is a feeling I have never known. A father, a mother, a friend, a woman...none of them ever offered me love! It's been a strange life...When I was young, I wanted to find my mother: that was my only ambition. And when that failed, everything else inside me died. Longing, desire, love...all the things that make up a life were never there for me. I never thought of having a job, a house, a family, a place in life, friends. But I don't have any bitterness. I'm free. Oh, but I'm a prisoner of my freedom. Yes, sir, as mad as it may seem, my freedom is a chain.'

Sadness darkened the old man's wild eyebrows and sparkling eyes. He lit a suruttu and exhaled bitter smoke that covered his sombre expression, then coughed raspingly, tapping his chest with his fist. Lourdes ran to him with a glass of water. He thanked her, but didn't drink it. He put it on a stool and picked up his glass of whisky.

'Thank you, dear. Water is good for the body but not the soul. This, this does your soul good!' As if waking from a dream, he slowly returned to his story.

'When I got to India, I only had an address written on a yellowed envelope. My father must have opened and closed it many times. I kept it in my pocket. It was my only hope...

'A few days later, I hired an old car that went as far as the entrance to a little village. The driver refused to go any further. He said that there was a cart blocking the way in. So he turned off the motor and went to relieve himself in the rice fields. It was late in the afternoon, and the village seemed to be sleeping deeply in the heat. Lazy dogs were lying under the trees. They looked at me but didn't bark. The noise of the vehicle, however, had caught the attention of some children, who began to swarm noisily around it. Cars were still rare and fascinating things in such a place. The few adults sitting in their thinnais looked at me with astonishment. They covered their brows with their hands to keep out the sun, but I could see the piercing looks on their faces.

'In my right hand I had my suitcase, and in my left a hat I used to fan myself. I began to walk down a narrow road where the houses had no numbers. Anyway, the envelope only had the name of the sender and of the village. I was filled with anxiety. I was lost in this tiny village. I looked around hoping to find someone who could help me. No one moved.

'I walked towards a young man who was standing in front of a house. I handed him the envelope. He took it, turned it over and over again, and asked me something in a language I didn't understand. He looked at me, not knowing what to do. His eyebrows rose and fell. I said that I was looking for someone and pointed to the name on the envelope. He stared at it for a while and then bobbed his head. I was confused. Was it a yes or a no? This was the first time I had seen this goddamn gesture! He saw what a pathetic shape I was in and called the neighbours.

'Soon a dozen people were standing around me. The envelope passed from one hand to another, but no one could tell me anything about the house I was looking for. They were talking loudly, waving their hands, laughing or looking at me suspiciously. I got fed up. I snatched the envelope from them and went back towards the car. The driver had returned from the fields and was busy chasing off the children who had gotten into the car

'But a toothless old man waved to me. I followed him – and the villagers followed me – towards a big house at the end of the road.

'A young man was sleeping in the thinnai of the house. He woke up suddenly and got to his feet in a clumsy motion. He took off his turban, tucked it under his left armpit and greeted me with an excessive bow.

'The crowd said something to him and he began to scrutinize me. He stood for a moment scratching his head. The old man who had brought me added something in an insistent voice, and the young man knocked nervously on the door of the house. After a moment as long as eternity, a woman came to the door. Opening it halfway, she looked past the villagers and then noticed me. Her face didn't show much, but she seemed exasperated. She spoke to the young man, but before he could respond I moved towards her and handed her the envelope. She stared at me, took it and closed the door behind her.

'Everyone waited without moving, unwilling to leave without finding out who this mysterious stranger was. The villagers whispered to each other and glanced furtively at me. The young man in the thinnai gestured for me to sit down, and took my suitcase from me. He set it down carefully after dusting the thinnai. He stood next to me uncomfortably, shifting his weight from one leg to the other and offering me an embarrassed grin. I returned an awkward smile. I was exhausted from the journey, the heat, this unknown land and this painful ordeal.

'Suddenly the door opened. The woman gestured for me to come inside after whispering something to the young man. I turned to the old man to thank him, but he just bobbed his head, smiled and stayed where he was, waiting to see what would happen. The young man waved his hands dramatically to shoo away the gawking villagers.

'Behind the door I found my grandmother.

'She had changed. I had remembered a strong woman who sang me lullabies. Sitting on her lap looking into the black night sky, I would sail away through the clouds, chasing the moon. Love, a thirst for life, lit her face from within. I hardly recognized the ancient woman in front of me. Her eyes were smoking coals. In the shadowy room, she touched me, feeling my face to be certain it was me, the grandson who had been taken from her so many years ago.

'She reached out her hands to ask for my help to get up and cross the room. When she came to the courtyard, she began to shudder and had to lean an arm against the teak columns. She caught my glance as it moved over the corners of the house. She dropped my hand and told me in a dry voice: "She's not here."

'All my hopes vanished.

'Sita's curse was fitting. I was born dead. My life had no meaning. I was disoriented, disappointed... I didn't know what to do. Some sort of unseen evil kept me from making any decision. I took this road, wandering towards nowhere. It's been fifty years that I've gone on like this, walking in a void...'

Silence filled the thinnai. Gilbert Thaata was ashamed. Lourdes brought him another bottle, and his confusion disappeared as if by magic. He rubbed his hands together, then noticed my father looking at Little Gilbert.

'He's like me, sir. A vagabond. No family, no ties, no destiny. I found him on a railway station. I don't know if he was lost or abandoned. Something strange seemed to come from this child. We looked at each other for a moment, and that was enough for fate to bring us together. When I got on board the train, I felt him grip my leg. He's never left me since. I gave him my name and forgot my own.'

A screech followed by sobs interrupted Gilbert Thaata. A silhouette ran from Asamandi Baiyacaca Sonal's house.

'Ayio! He's gone! My *magaarasan* left me! Ayio, ayio! What will I do?' The koratti ran back and forth, beating her chest.

~

Gilbert Thaata was packing his bag as the first mourners came to the dead man's house. Their hair was dishevelled, their expressions pitiful. They hadn't even seen the body yet, but they were already weeping, beating their chests, pretending to faint and falling to the ground only to pick up handfuls of sand that they threw skyward, cursing the gods. Kelna, their leader, was the last to arrive. Her expression was stoic and severe, but as soon as she entered the house she fell at the dead man's feet, screaming in agony. The other women gathered around the corpse, joining her grief.

Their wailing was punctuated by the sound of the first wife's mortar and pestle. She refused to participate in the ceremony.

'You could have died in my arms, Jean-Noël,' the old woman wept to herself, unable to hold back her tears.

Little Gilbert was saying goodbye to Three-Balls Six-Faces and a few other friends gathered around the fountain. He didn't want to leave. He liked this neighbourhood, where he had made friends and had eaten well. He turned around and headed towards the thinnai. Those who follow the clouds have to bury their hearts.

'Would it be stupid of me to ask where you're headed, old-timer?' My father meant to ask this question with an air of detachment. He was surprised to hear his voice tremble. He coughed and lit a cigarette.

He would have liked it if the old man were to end his days in the thinnai. But Gilbert Thaata now felt that he had received a sacred mission: he must return the Stone of Sita to the temple from which it had been stolen. It was as if he had been struck by a revelation.

'You mean you still have the diamond?' My father couldn't believe it when the old man told him of his plan.

'Yes sir, the stone is still with me. At least, what's left of it... a few fragments to keep me alive.'

The lamentations of the koratti rose to heaven.

'Do you really have to go?'

'Sir, I can't escape fate. But let me give you something,' he said, fumbling in his pocket.

Little Gilbert picked up his sack. It had been a long time since he had felt its weight on his shoulders. The old man avoided his pleading gaze. Little Gilbert's legs trembled. The sack fell in the dirt. Gilbert Thaata's cane, after sitting for such a long time in the corner of the thinnai, fell once again on the boy's back.

While the two figures faded out of view on the road to Vaazhakulam, Selvanadin's father was coming to blows with the leader of the funeral musicians. No one could remember how it started, but every funeral ended with a fight between the two men. Last time, Selvanadin's father had been humiliated by the drummer, who had dragged him all around the neighbourhood. Now he wanted revenge. He seized the drummer by the leg while the musician struggled and kept beating his drum.

Manickam Annan was busy putting up posters for the next election. Monsieur Michel had been right to worry. The local Communist Party, taking advantage of Manickam Annan's new-found popularity, had nominated him as a candidate. They had taken over every wall in the neighbourhood: the teeth of the future gulag chief, painted an impossible white, beamed from the posters as if to sell toothpaste. When he saw the posters from which his rival smiled triumphantly flanked by Marx and Lenin, Monsieur Michel had a heart attack.

Gilbert Thaata turned at the end of the street for a last look back. Kurusukuppam disappeared.

14

'No, Paulin, not you! Don't tell me you fell for it, too!' The jeweller turned the stone between his thumb and index finger.

'It can't be true, sethji! Look carefully, are you sure?' My father was astonished and disappointed.

The old Marwari jeweller knew diamonds, and everyone knew him to be an honest man.

'You're not the first, Paulin.' He bent down and spat beeda into a copper bowl. He wiped the corner of his mouth and set the stone upon a blue velvet cloth. 'Let me guess... This is a piece of the Stone of Sita. It disappeared during the French Revolution. Then it reappeared in the Caribbean. And then...'

'Stop, sethji, that's enough. You know the story.' My father was furious and sad. Had Gilbert Thaata really made it all up? Had people lost all dignity and kindness?

My father picked up the stone and held it in his palm.

'So, he was just a common cheat?'

'We don't know if he's a sharp dealer, Paulin, or just a fool.'

'And the Stone of Sita?'

'Will keep its secrets.'

EPILOGUE

The man drew near with hesitant steps. He held his arms behind his back, and his gait was strange. Slow and limping footfalls betrayed his reluctance. For a moment that seemed as long as an eternity, he stopped beneath the lamp post. He meant to speak to the group of boys mocking him. A stone whistled past his ears, crashing against the wall of the thinnai. Emile Kozhukattai-Head shot out a curse, angry that he had missed his target, as his friends doubled over in laughter. Three-Balls Six-Faces left his seat on the big thinnai and settled down beside me.

'Whatever you do, keep away from him!' he whispered to me, pointing with his chin to the man making his way towards us. He saw my surprise; his face was twisted in a grimace of contempt. 'Watch out, he's a leper,' he warned.

'Come on, friend, come on. It's time to finally get rid of you.' Three-Balls Six-Faces took cruel pleasure in giving the bad news. 'The owner of the house is back from France, you see. He's going to tear down this shack and build a new house.

There's nothing you can do but take your things and run off. You can't play your clever little tricks anymore.' Then he turned to me. 'Yes, because monsieur doesn't want to leave the thinnai, no matter how much the neighbours complain. He refused to leave until the owners came to ask him in person. He's been telling us about laws and rules, as if he were a lawyer. Go on, tell him yourself. Tell him to take his bags...'

Ignoring Three-Balls Six-Faces' litany, I smiled at the man, who wavered at the edge of the thinnai. His dangling, stumpy arms were trembling; he didn't know how to hide them. He gripped the tundu that slid over his torso and tried to cover his shoulders. His face, wasted by his illness, had an awkward smile. He raised his crippled hand in a military salute addressed to me. After I invited him into the thinnai, he sat down facing me, carefully hiding his bandaged feet beneath his kaili. He seemed more at ease and, taking out a beedi, began to smoke.

'Perhaps you would prefer a cigarette?' I said, offering him my packet, as Three-Balls Six-Faces watched in horror.

Cigarette smoke rose lazily above the big thinnai. As he relaxed, the man looked me over slowly and said: 'My name is De Cruz, Oliveira de Cruz. But the neighbours call me Digriss...'